HA... ...HED HIS MURDER

MARGOT KINGSLEY: The amorous young widow topped the list of suspects. Her husband's passing brought her freedom—and pots of lovely money. She had millions in motive, but no opportunity . . .

SIMON BARNES: Kingsley had threatened to expose his secret. But there was more than Simon's dubious reputation at stake . . .

MICK CORCORAN: The red-haired stranger had an appointment with the deceased. He also had a good alibi. In fact, it was a trifle *too* good . . .

VEEDA RILEY: She was the late Julian Kingsley's past mistress, a businesswoman who could put a generous legacy to very profitable use . . .

ANTON SZABO: Hot-headed and coolly calculating, the festival's director-designer was ruled by ambition. And the only one with more power than himself was . . . dead!

JAMES HALL: The police have him cast as the merry widow's mystery lover. Motive, opportunity—the frame fits, but Jane *has* to believe her husband is innocent!

DEADLY REHEARSAL

Books by Audrey Peterson

Deadly Rehearsal
Death in Wessex
Murder in Burgundy
The Nocturne Murder

Published by POCKET BOOKS

DEADLY REHEARSAL

Audrey Peterson

POCKET BOOKS

New York   London   Toronto   Sydney   Tokyo   Singapore

An *Original* Publication of POCKET BOOKS

POCKET BOOKS, a division of Simon & Schuster Inc.
1230 Avenue of the Americas, New York, NY 10020

ISBN: 0-671-69169-4

First Pocket Books printing May 1990

10 9 8 7 6 5 4 3 2 1

POCKET and colophon are registered trademarks of
Simon & Schuster Inc.

Printed in the U.S.A.

For R.L.B.

1

Standing in the wings of the Southmere Festival Theater in Sussex, I was watching the dress rehearsal of the new production of *La Traviata*. The glamorous young soprano, Ilena Santos, as Violetta, had just sung the first portion of her aria, *"Ah, fors' è lui"*—asking herself if true love was possible—when in a moment of silence, the voice of Margot Kingsley rang out.

"Then go! I don't give a damn what you do!"

Startled, Ilena looked up at the Kingsleys' box, then smoothly picked up her cue and went on.

Only minutes after the end of the act, I heard the first fluttering whisper of trouble.

"Julian . . . It's Mr. Kingsley . . . Something's gone wrong—"

Someone clutched my arm and I heard my friend Bettina's voice. "Oh, Jane—it's Uncle Julian. They say he's been hurt."

"Where?"

"I don't know. Outdoors, someone said."

In the backstage dusk, I could just make out the fear in Bettina's enormous eyes. My sweet, capable friend was looking scattered and disoriented.

1

I quickly made for the stage door exit. Outside, in the darkness, the cold October air bit into my cheeks as we hurried after a figure loping down the path through the gardens toward the car park. I heard footsteps behind us and saw that two members of the stage crew had joined the procession.

A quavery voice cried out, "Up here, by the tower!" and we all veered off, running up the path toward the immense blackness of the old stone tower that stood on the hill above the grounds of Southmere.

As we reached the walk that skirted the tower, I saw a body sprawled awkwardly on the ancient stones, and even in the dark I could see that it was Julian Kingsley, the impresario of the festival.

Alfred, the old servant of the Southmere household, who was acting as stage doorman for the dress rehearsal, sat with Julian's head cradled in his lap.

Bettina knelt down. "What happened, Alfred?"

"We don't know, Miss Bettina." All ladies, married or single, were *miss* to Alfred. "The gentleman as found 'im 'as gone to fetch the ambulance."

"Uncle Julian—can you hear me?" Bettina gently touched her uncle's face, then pulled back her hand. "Oh, Jane, is he—?"

I doubted that I would know any better than she whether he was alive or dead, but I knelt down and reached for Julian's wrist. His icy hand gave no sign of a pulse, but I was no nurse.

I looked at Alfred. "Has he spoken since you came?" I asked.

"Not a word, Miss Jane." His woeful eyes met mine over Bettina's bent head.

"Who found him?" I asked.

"Your 'usband found 'im, Miss Jane, and went to use the phone."

"James found him? Then where is he?"

2

"He's waiting in the drive, miss, to direct the crew when they come."

Then we heard the sound of the approaching ambulance and moved aside as the men came with their stretcher to take Julian Kingsley away.

By the time Bettina and I got back to the theater, the sets had been changed and Act Two had begun. From backstage, I looked out into the darkened house, where at last I saw my husband James. He had approached the podium and was speaking softly to Russell Ames, the conductor, who stared at James, then dropped his arm, tapping his baton for silence.

"Good God!" I heard Russell exclaim. He murmured something to James, and they both looked up at the end box on the second tier, which hung nearly over the stage.

"Margot!" Russell called softly.

A hand pushed aside the red plush curtain of the box and the head of Margot Kingsley appeared, her thick fair hair, fashionably silvered, swinging over her face. "What is it, darling?"

Russell cleared his throat. "You'd best come down, Margot." He turned to James. "Will you—?"

"Yes, of course."

As the music resumed, I saw James turn and walk toward the foyer where Margot would descend from the box. Planning to meet him, I went through the door leading from the stage into the foyer, along the carpeted passage, and around the corner, where I stopped abruptly. Twenty feet away, at the bottom of the staircase, James and Margot stood wrapped in each other's arms. Her head was on his shoulder, her arms clasped at his neck.

Stunned, I stood staring. A pounding pain began in

my chest. Then James turned his head and saw me, a deep flush mottling his face.

I walked swiftly back along the passage, opened a side door, and fled into the darkness of the walled garden. Pacing beside the tall cypresses, I muttered to myself, like a litany. "No, not James, not my darling, no, not James . . ."

Of course I knew that James and Margot had once been lovers. It had been before I came to London from the States and met him, before Margot married Julian Kingsley. I knew that James had been terribly in love with her, that she had treated him badly for nearly two years, and had finally left him for someone else. Julian came later on.

When Bettina, who ran the business end of the festival for her uncle Julian Kingsley, offered me a job as publicist on the project, handling press releases and assorted duties, James and I had talked about the inevitability of his seeing Margot. He had laughed and said that meeting Margot again would mean nothing to him.

"One look at her, darling, will only make me happier than ever that I found you!"

Now I stopped pacing and sank onto a stone bench, leaning my head against a marble statue of a water nymph.

"Jane! Are you there?"

Black clouds slid away from the moon, and in the watery light I saw a figure hurrying down the gravel path toward me and heard the soft swoosh of pebbles. Then James was there, holding me and stroking my hair.

"Oh, Jane—my dearest love. It wasn't what you think. I know how it must have looked—but poor Margot was dreadfully upset. I told her Julian had been taken to the hospital and she staggered and

4

nearly fell. She threw her arms round my neck and I held her for support. She's rather emotional, you see—"

I'd seen enough of Margot in the past two weeks to know she dramatized everything. I suppose I shouldn't have doubted James, except that any man might find the glamorous Margot irresistible. And after all, he *had* loved her once.

I managed a shaky laugh, and as we went along together toward the theater, I suddenly remembered to ask James what had happened to Julian.

He frowned. "I don't know. I thought he might have had a heart attack, but he was absolutely still, and so sort of sprawled out, as if he had fallen—"

"Yes, Bettina and I saw him before the ambulance came. But, James, how did you happen to find him?"

"It was quite by chance. When I drove into the parking lot, following your directions, I felt a bit cramped after the drive down from London, so I strolled up the path toward the tower. Just to stretch my legs, you see—"

My heart gave a slight lurch. Was he getting up the courage to see Margot again? I must stop this.

"Yes, of course," I murmured.

"I saw someone lying on the walk at the foot of the tower, and of course, when I bent over, I recognized Kingsley from photographs I've seen, so I dashed down toward the theater, found the stage door, and rang up for the ambulance."

It wouldn't be hard to identify Julian, I thought. As a handsome and distinguished patron of the arts, and founder of the Southmere Festival Theater, Julian was often pictured in the press.

I said, "Julian and Margot were having a flaming row during the first act. When the music stopped, everyone could hear them."

James made no reply, and when we reached the stage door we found old Alfred back at his post.

"Any news of Mr. Kingsley?" I asked.

"No, miss."

"And Mrs. Kingsley?" I forced myself to add.

"Mr. Simon took her along to the hospital."

As we moved away, I murmured to James, "At least, Simon's found something useful to do."

Bettina's husband, Simon Barnes, was one of those good-looking, glib young men who hang about doing nothing and looking immensely pleased with themselves. He was engaged in some sort of transport and haulage business, but his attendance to his duties seemed to be spasmodic at best.

Now I said, "Let's go out front," and we slipped quietly into the ground floor stalls and took a couple of seats halfway up the center aisle.

2

This was James's first view of the interior of the Southmere Theater, and I saw him smile at its rococo charm. Julian Kingsley's father, an ardent theater buff, had devoted a chunk of the family millions to creating this exquisite little house after the horseshoe pattern of the European court theaters. Three gallery tiers, each with its curtained boxes in classic red plush, sprouted gilt cupids, shaded lamps, and ornamental carvings. Some concessions to modernity had been made—the ground floor sloped for better sight lines, and backstage space was reasonably generous—but during the father's lifetime, the theater had remained a hobby, where private performances were given for family and friends.

It was Julian, the opera enthusiast, who had decided, after his father's death, to go public, somewhat in the pattern of his famous neighbor at Glyndebourne, thirty miles or so west of Southmere. In this, the third season, Julian was presenting two operas over a ten-day period, opening the festival the next evening with Benjamin Britten's *The Turn of the Screw*.

The Southmere Theater held only four hundred

7

seats, with almost no room for expansion, so that even with high ticket prices, Julian picked up an enormous tab each season and was hot on the trail of outside financing to ease the burden.

Now, as James and I watched the second act of *Traviata*, Alfredo was singing of the rapture of his love for Violetta, Verdi's lush music sounding rather incongruous in the trendy setting created by Anton Szabo, the Hungarian designer-director. As a subscriber to the current craze for the bizarre in opera staging, Szabo had updated the opera to contemporary Paris, making Violetta a cheap prostitute instead of an elegantly kept lady of the camellias.

Looking around the darkened house, I saw Ilena's husband, the American psychiatrist Raymond Flynt, across the aisle. He flapped a hand in return to my wave, his mouthful of teeth emerging from the surrounding beard in the broad grin he habitually wore. Raymond always looked to me as if he had just arrived at a surprise party given in his honor and couldn't quite believe his luck.

When Alfredo left the stage and his father, Germont, was announced, Anton Szabo suddenly shouted from behind us at the singer playing the bit part of Giuseppi, Violetta's servant. A local who had been recruited to fill in at the last moment in this minor role, he had not been at previous rehearsals.

"No, no! Stop!" Anton came down the aisle, waving his arms and shaking his head full of black curls, his body electric with vitality.

Russell Ames looked exasperated but dutifully rapped and the orchestra faded.

"Don't act so damned respectful," Anton called out to the singer. "You are *not* a servant, for Christ's sake! I don't give a shit what Verdi's libretto says. You live in the shack next door and your attitude is, 'This guy says he's Alfredo's father—so what?' "

Anton may have been born in Hungary, but he had lived in the States since the age of fourteen and sounded more American than I did.

The singer did his best with the direction, and the rehearsal moved on to the scene in which Germont, sung by the up-and-coming baritone, Riccardo Palma, persuades Violetta to sacrifice herself for Alfredo's sake. Even in traditional productions of *La Traviata,* I had always had some trouble believing that Alfredo's having a liaison with a woman of questionable virtue would cause his sister's fiancé to break off their engagement. By moving the opera from the nineteenth century to the 1980s, Anton had made this situation truly absurd.

The singers were in top voice as the rehearsal moved along. During scene changes, we chatted with the doctor, who beamed joyfully through his beard at us.

It must have been about half-past eight, two hours after the rehearsal began, when we suddenly heard loud voices behind us. Turning, we saw two uniformed policemen, with Anton Szabo at their heels, approach the conductor, who again stopped the rehearsal.

Now Russell Ames raised his voice. "Ladies and gentlemen. I have just been informed that Mr. Julian Kingsley was pronounced dead on arrival at the hospital in Burling. The police are here. Will everyone in the theater please assemble on the stage?"

Amid sounds of shock and distress, the singers, the chorus, the musicians, the dressers, the stage crew, and the rest of us milled about on the stage, finally settling into a vague semicircle facing the police officers, who stood down center. Good thing this production requires a really stripped-down chorus and orchestra, I thought, or not all of us would fit on the stage at once.

James and I stood with Bettina, her huge eyes brimming with tears. "Poor Uncle Julian. I was afraid—that is, he did look so dreadful, Jane, didn't he?"

I nodded and squeezed her hand.

"Thank you, ladies and gentlemen. I am Sergeant Glenn of the Burling Police Department. With me is Constable Hopkins. As you have been informed, Mr. Julian Kingsley was pronounced dead on arrival at the hospital. His body was found here on the grounds of Southmere. The preliminary medical examination has indicated that owing to the appearance of multiple fractures throughout the body of the deceased, the death may have been the result of a fall from a considerable height. Directly above the spot on the walk where the body was found, there is a small terrace or balcony on the tower, approximately forty feet from the ground, and it is possible that Mr. Kingsley fell from there to his death.

"As you know, any death from an unexplained cause must be investigated by the police. In this case, the death may be the result of accident, of suicide, or, if the deceased was pushed from the tower by another person, of homicide."

"But that is ridiculous!" Ilena's throaty voice rang out. "Why would anyone wish to kill poor Julian? Such a kind man, such a dear man—"

Surreptitious glances were exchanged but no one spoke. Julian had been a powerful, even magnetic, personality, but "kind" and "dear" were not the adjectives that sprang to the lips when one thought of him. Ilena's husband, Raymond Flynt, patted her hand, his fixed grin looking oddly out of place in the circumstances.

Now the sound of rapid footsteps came from stage

right, and Margot Kingsley, followed by Simon Barnes, burst onto the stage. She paused dramatically, stared at the policemen and the assembled group, gasped slightly, then ran straight toward James and threw herself into his arms.

Not again, I wanted to shout! Come off it, Margot. But I restrained myself; after all, the woman's husband had just died.

"Oh, James, isn't it dreadful?" Margot was moaning, her head on his shoulder in the now-familiar pose.

Sergeant Glenn cleared his throat. "Excuse me, madam."

Margot disentangled herself from James and swung her silver blonde hair in the direction of the sergeant. "Yes, of course. So sorry."

"Do you feel able to answer a few questions, madam?"

"Yes, I'll try."

Someone gave Margot a chair and she sank down, crossing her legs, her back so straight it almost arched. In her tight jeans and baggy sweater she managed to look as seductive as Ilena in her sexy satin gown.

"First," the sergeant began, "is it your wish, madam, that tonight's rehearsal should continue?"

Margot looked almost surprised. Then she lowered her eyes and produced a sort of strangled sob. "Yes, Sergeant. I know my husband would want everything to go on as planned. The festival was dreadfully important to him, you see."

"Thank you, madam. In that case, I shall ask a few questions before the rehearsal resumes. May I ask that no one leave the theater until all further questioning has been concluded?"

Now we all looked at the sergeant like a group of school children waiting for the teacher to begin the lesson.

11

3

Sergeant Glenn began with a question about the time at which Julian Kingsley was last seen. Eyes swivelled toward Margot, who gave a little choke, then spoke in a voice which seemed to be suppressing tears.

"We were sitting up there in the box, watching the rehearsal. Actually, Sergeant, we were having a bit of a row. It was quite unimportant, really. Then Julian left and went down the stairs."

"At what time was this, madam?"

"Oh, it must have been shortly before seven o'clock. He'd been consulting his watch and muttering about meeting someone at seven."

"Did Mr. Kingsley name the person he expected to meet?"

Margot dropped her eyes, then looked directly at the sergeant. "No. I rather thought it must be a member of the press, but it could have been anyone. Masses of people were always hanging about."

This was absurd, as everyone but the sergeant knew. Either Bettina or I usually met the press people first, and the London critics were not due until the following

12

evening for the opening performance. Otherwise, at this hour there was almost no one around.

"I see. Can anyone confirm the time Mr. Kingsley left the box?"

There was a murmur of voices. I had seen Margot and Julian myself, and had certainly heard their voices raised in anger, but I wasn't sure what time it was when Margot had cried out, "Go, then. I don't give a damn what you do!"

Several people confirmed Julian's presence but no one quoted Margot's words to the sergeant, although a good many of us must have heard her. One or two people thought it must have been close to seven o'clock when they heard Margot's and Julian's voices, but no one seemed sure of the time until Anton Szabo spoke. Directing a venomous glance at Margot, he said, "I believe I can tell you the time, Sergeant. It was shortly before seven o'clock when I heard Mrs. Kingsley—er—tell her husband to leave her."

"And did he reply?"

"He muttered something in an angry tone, but I didn't catch the words."

"And where were you, sir, at this time?"

"Actually, I was standing almost directly below the box where they sat."

Margot stared at Anton, then said in a voice icy with contempt, "I wasn't aware that Mr. Szabo kept a log of our movements."

Everyone knew there was little love lost between those two. Margot habitually referred scathingly to Anton as the Hungarian genius, and, outside Julian's hearing, he called her the Blond Bitch.

Sergeant Glenn asked Anton, "How does it happen that you recall the time, sir?"

"I had gone up to the second tier to check the lighting effects, and when I came back down, I looked at my watch to see how the timing was going. It was then just before seven. I could hear the voices of Mr. and Mrs. Kingsley above me."

I wondered how long it would be before Anton told the police in detail about the quarrel between Margot and Julian. I suspected he wouldn't pass up a chance to annoy her, pointless though it might be.

The sergeant asked if anyone had seen Julian after he left the box and was greeted with utter silence. Then he glanced at his notes and turned to James.

"Mr. Hall, will you please describe how you came to find the body of Mr. Kingsley?"

"Yes, certainly. I drove down from London—"

"At what time did you leave?"

"Let me see. I left my office in London at about four o'clock."

"You are a solicitor?"

"Yes. In the Grays Inn. I went home to our flat, fixed myself a sandwich, and set off to drive down here to Sussex. It must have been some time after four o'clock when I left the flat. The traffic coming out of London on a Friday afternoon is extremely congested."

James described going into the parking lot at Southmere, walking up toward the tower, and seeing someone lying on the stone walk. "I saw that it was Mr. Kingsley and thought he might have suffered a heart attack or something of the sort. I hurried down the hill and found the stage door of the theater, and rang up for an ambulance. It was then after seven o'clock, I should think."

The sergeant again glanced at his notes. "Yes. The call was placed at eleven minutes past seven. Is there anyone present who saw Mr. Kingsley between the time he left the theater box and the time he was found by Mr. Hall?"

14

Again, silence.

"Thank you, ladies and gentlemen. If any one recalls anything that might shed light upon this—er—tragedy, please make it known to us."

Five minutes later, the rehearsal had resumed and Sergeant Glenn was closeted with Margot in a small cubicle near the stage door, the only place available for his interviews. Ordinarily, several dressing rooms would have been empty, but as this was a dress rehearsal, all the rooms were in use. Not that the dressers in this production had the usual problems in *La Traviata* with the elaborately hooped skirts for Violetta and her friends in the first two acts, but even the tattiest costumes had to be changed.

Backstage, some of us stood in a little group, Bettina with her arm around Simon, Raymond watching his wife Ilena sing, seemingly in rapt astonishment, except that he always looked like that.

"Poor Margot." Bettina looked toward the cubicle where Margot and the sergeant were visible through the glass. "She's bearing up wonderfully."

Raymond tore his eyes away from his wife. "Right! But Margot's bound to be traumatized. Especially because she and Julian were quarreling just before he died. People often have trouble resolving their conflicts in cases like that. I once had a patient who—"

Simon, who had been tossing his car keys from hand to hand, dropped them on the floor and managed to step on Raymond's foot as he retrieved them.

"So sorry, Raymond. Awfully clumsy of me."

Irritating as Simon often was, I couldn't help being amused at his ploy in cutting Raymond off at the pass. Thinking I might as well take advantage of it, I put in, "What took you and Margot so long to get back from the hospital, Simon?"

Simon gave me his most charming smile. "They kept us hanging about for ages, waiting for the doctor to give Margot the bad news. Did you know they never say anyone died? This one hemmed and hawed and finally came out with 'expired.' When we left, Margot said, 'For God's sake, let's stop somewhere for a drink,' and we nipped into a pub for a couple of stiff ones."

Bettina gave Simon one of her adoring looks. "That was wonderful of you, darling."

I never ceased to wonder that my dear friend Bettina had never caught on that Simon was the phony I believed him to be. Her Uncle Julian had spotted it at once and made it clear to her two years ago that if she married Simon, he would cut her out of his will. Since he had also made this clear to Simon, I was surprised that Simon married her after all, instead of fading out of the picture as I'm sure Julian expected him to do.

Now Margot emerged from the booth and Bettina was summoned by Constable Hopkins to take her place. I saw the glitter in Margot's eye as she came toward us, her arms extended, and I promptly stepped in front of James. Three times in one evening would have been too much for me. Thwarted, Margot threw herself at Simon, who obligingly embraced her and began patting her on the shoulder, crooning, "Poor Margot, brave girl."

Looking solicitously at Margot, Bettina asked, "Was it dreadful being questioned, poor darling?"

Detaching herself from Simon, Margot almost smiled. "Not really. Actually, the sergeant is an absolute duck." Then, remembering that she ought to be stricken, she added, "He wanted to know if Julian could have taken his own life, and I said I thought it was unlikely and that it must have been an accident.

16

Of course, it's all been perfectly ghastly. Simon, will you be a dear and see me back to the house?"

"Yes, of course, love." Simon put his arm around Margot and together they went slowly through the door from the stage into the foyer, from where it was a walk of fifty yards or so to the main house.

"Stay with Margot, darling," Bettina called after Simon. Then to us, "I'm glad Simon and I are staying at the house. Otherwise, poor Margot would be alone except for the servants."

I knew Margot had decreed that only Bettina and Simon, who after all were family, might stay at the house during the festival, while its twelve other bedrooms remained empty. Some of the cast elected to commute from London, while those of us who wanted to stay over had found lodging among the local hotels and guest houses. Anton Szabo, in his antisocial way, had taken a cottage on the road above Southmere.

"It's impossible to get really good help," Margot had declared, according to Bettina. "If Julian must pursue his hobby, there's no reason why the house should be turned upside down."

When Margot and Simon departed, I was about to make a nasty crack to James about Margot's dramatics, when he astonished me by saying, "Poor Margot. She's dreadfully cut up about Julian. She was quite devoted to him."

I looked into James's clear blue eyes and saw only genuine concern. Was this really my beloved, my dear husband who, as a solicitor, had seen just about everything human nature had to offer and was rarely duped by anyone? Did he really fall for Margot's act and believe she was grieving deeply? Or was I being unfair, believing that Margot was incapable of caring for anyone but herself?

A commotion at the stage door drew our attention.

A uniformed policeman whom we hadn't seen before was urging forward a man with vivid red hair. As they came into the wings, the officer said to Constable Hopkins, "I found this gent hanging about up by the tower, Bert, so I brought him along."

The red-haired man snapped, "I wasn't hanging about. I had an appointment with Mr. Julian Kingsley."

Hopkins looked grave. "Your name, sir?"

"Mick Corcoran, if you must know. But what's all the fuss? This officer refused to tell me what's going on."

"The fact is, sir, Mr. Julian Kingsley is dead."

Mick Corcoran whistled. "Dead, eh? That's a turnup! But it's nothing to do with me!"

4

In the end, it was after ten o'clock before James and I left the theater that evening. By keeping further interruptions to a necessary minimum, the conductor Russell Ames had managed to end the rehearsal in good time, with Anton Szabo cooperating for once and not hectoring everyone in sight over details of dubious importance. There had after all been three weeks of rehearsals with the principals, a luxury which Julian had insisted upon and which the large opera houses of the world could rarely achieve. By using young singers from all over the world who were on their way up, the Southmere Festival could require more rehearsal time than the big name performers could give, with the added bonus of good looks and talented acting on the part of the singers.

After a long interview with Bettina, Sergeant Glenn had spoken with the red-haired stranger, Mick Corcoran, who was then allowed to go. Next were various members of the stage crew: old Alfred at the stage door and the singers as they were available. He spoke with Ilena before Act Three began, and with Dmitri Mikos before his entrance in that act. The singers taking the supporting roles of Flora and the Baron, who were on stage during the critical time, were briefly interviewed, followed by the baritone, Riccardo Palma.

After his session, Riccardo came out to chat with us while waiting for his final entrance near the end of the opera. So skillful was his makeup as Germont, Alfredo's father, that I had to remind myself, even at close range, that this seemingly gray-haired man with the lined face was really a young man of twenty-eight.

When I introduced them, Riccardo shook James's hand with Italian gusto. "So this is the husband of our lovely Jane! When she speaks of you, the stars come into her eyes!" Riccardo gave me a theatrical hug and kiss on the cheek.

"Your second act was marvelous, Riccardo," I said, with genuine admiration.

"Ah, yes. The voice is good tonight, I think." Singers always spoke of "the voice" as if it were some kind of wild creature outside themselves over which they had only dubious control. Sometimes it was chained and docile; at other times it misbehaved, straining against the leash of discipline.

Eyes glittering, Riccardo now launched into the topic of Julian's untimely death. "The sergeant looked at me very suspicious-like when he learned that I am not on stage when poor Mr. Kingsley dies. As if I would have any reason to push him off the tower! He is my benefactor. He gives me the role of Germont, he pays us all better than we expect. I hope for future benefits from him. So why should I kill him, I ask you?"

"I'm sure no one seriously suspects you, Riccardo," I soothed.

Lowering his voice to the confidential whisper of the confirmed gossip, Riccardo cast his liquid dark eyes upon both of us. "I overhear something one day, but I do not tell the sergeant. Tell me if I do right. I am hurrying from the parking area in to rehearsal of Act Two, and I am humming to warm up the voice, when I hear Mr. Kingsley shouting, very angry at someone. As I round the corner, I see that it is Simon Barnes, the husband of our dear Bettina. Simon say, 'There is nothing to find out,' and Mr. Kingsley say, 'Never mind how long it takes, I'll get to the bottom of this!' Did I do right not to tell the sergeant?"

I looked at James, who thought for a moment, then asked, "Was that all you heard, Riccardo? No other details?"

"That is all."

"Then I see no point in mentioning it to the police. It doesn't actually constitute a motive for murder, does it?"

Riccardo looked shocked. "Oh, no, I do not intend—that is, I never meant—"

I said, "I'm sure you didn't." And Riccardo scurried off to his dressing room.

Meanwhile, Anton Szabo was interviewed, followed by Ilena's husband, Raymond Flynt. When Raymond emerged from his session, white teeth gleaming through the surrounding thicket of hair, he pulled up a chair next to where James and I sat meekly awaiting our turn.

"So, how was the inquisition?" I asked Raymond.

He beamed. "Whaddya know?" Raymond liked to indulge in folksy phrases, no doubt designed to assure his patients that he was not a formidable psychiatrist but just one of the boys. "I think the sergeant actually believes somebody might have pushed poor old Julian off that balcony in the tower!"

James said, "That *is* one of the possibilities, along with accident or suicide."

21

Raymond chuckled. "Yes, but how would anybody get Julian to go up inside the tower at night, in the middle of the dress rehearsal?"

This was exactly the question that James and I had been pondering. Since Julian had been a man who antagonized people right and left, plenty of people disliked him, although I had admitted to James that ruffled feathers were hardly a likely motive for murder. But, granting that someone did want to kill him, I couldn't see for the life of me why Julian would put himself out to climb the stairs to the balcony, when the meeting could take place at the bottom of the tower.

"After all," I had said to James, "Julian evidently had an appointment with the red-haired fellow Corcoran at the *base* of the tower, not up above!"

Now it was my turn and I was summoned to the cubicle. I was pleased to find Sergeant Glenn a pleasant and courteous young man.

He began with a question about my name, which he found understandably puzzling. "You are Miss Jane Winfield?"

"Yes."

"And you are married to Mr. James Hall?"

I smiled. "Yes. I still use my professional name, since I'm a freelance writer, but I'm frequently addressed as Mrs. Hall, and either name is fine."

"I see. And how long have you been acquainted with the deceased?"

"I first met Mr. Kingsley about four months ago, when I was asked to do the publicity for the two operas at this year's festival, and to help my friend Bettina Barnes with her administrative duties."

"What sort of writing do you do, Miss Winfield?"

"I write reviews and articles on music and I've published a biography of a nineteenth-century English

22

composer. I'm presently working on a biography of an American impresario in collaboration with my former professor, Dr. Andrew Quentin."

"I see. And how did you first meet Mr. Kingsley?"

"I met Julian when Mrs. Barnes invited me to lunch in London to confer with her uncle, and I evidently met with his approval, as I was hired soon afterward. I did a lot of preliminary work in London, and I've been here in Sussex off and on for the past two weeks."

The sergeant wrote deftly in his notebook, then went on. "Will you please describe the sort of person Mr. Kingsley was, in your opinion?"

I paused. "I assume that platitudes will be of little help to you, sergeant. Julian was a strong personality. To speak frankly, he was egotistical and impatient, and many people found him difficult to deal with. Perhaps growing up with enormous wealth gave him a certain arrogance that he may not have been fully aware of. At the same time, he was dedicated to the success of the opera festival here at Southmere, and I admired him for that. We got along well enough because I didn't allow his brusque manner to intimidate me, and he obviously liked that. He could be rather cruel to anyone who trembled under his gaze, so to speak."

"Thank you. Do you believe Mr. Kingsley might have taken his own life for any reason?"

"I should think it's extremely unlikely. Julian was intensely involved in the festival. It was almost an obsession with him. The past two seasons have been a marvelous start, and this year we are totally booked, except for the usual number of seats held for last moment VIPs. Julian would scarcely have taken his own life at such a time."

"Yes, this seems to be generally agreed upon by everyone who knew Mr. Kingsley. Now, will you describe when you last saw the deceased?"

"Yes. The rehearsal began at half-past six, and during the first ten minutes or so, I sat in the stalls watching, as I had no official duties this evening. Julian Kingsley was in the end box on the second tier, as you know. Shortly after the rehearsal began, Margot—Mrs. Kingsley—joined her husband in the box. She's not an opera enthusiast, as you may have learned, and I could see that she was angry with her husband about something. Her voice was low at first, and he gestured to her to be quiet. She was silent for a time, then began speaking to him again, her voice louder than before.

"About twenty minutes to seven, I left the stalls and went through to the wings on this side of the stage. I was expecting my husband, and though I had no idea what time he would get away from his office, I thought he might come as early as seven o'clock. I'd told him to come to the stage door, as the front of the house is usually locked after dark.

"At a pause in the music, I heard more sounds of the quarrel. From where I was standing in the wings, I could see Margot's head over the edge of the box as she leaned toward her husband, who was behind the curtain. A few minutes later, at another pause, we heard Margot—er—tell Julian to leave."

Impassive, the sergeant merely said, "Yes, so I understand."

I confirmed that the time must have been shortly before seven, although I had become absorbed in the performance and couldn't be sure.

Then the sergeant asked a question which surprised me. "Do you know of your own knowledge whether

Mr. Kingsley was in the habit of using any sort of drugs?"

I confess I looked startled, not because I would have been shocked at the knowledge—using marijuana and cocaine were common enough in the circles of people like Margot and Julian—but because I had never thought of it in connection with Julian. His mood swings had seemed natural enough for someone with his tempestuous nature. Now, in answer to the sergeant's question, I simply said that I knew nothing about it, one way or the other.

After a few more routine questions, Sergeant Glenn thanked me and at last asked me to send James to him. It seemed odd to me that we had not both been questioned earlier so that we might leave, but the sergeant had evidently left James for last.

When James emerged from the interview, the rehearsal had ended and we made our way to the nearly deserted parking area at the back of the theater. As we followed the drive which curved past the theater and the main house of Southmere and onto the road leading to the town of Burling a scant two miles away, I asked James how his session with the sergeant had gone.

"Oh, well enough. Of course I had to tell him I had known Margot long ago. Actually, I gathered she had already told him so herself. He pressed me about the time I arrived, how long I spent walking up toward the tower, and so on. I couldn't be very definite, as I hadn't really noticed the time. Then he asked again if I had ever met Julian before, and when I said I had not, he asked how I knew it was he when I found him lying on the walk. I explained that I'd seen his picture in the press on more than one occasion, and he sort of raised a polite eyebrow and said, 'I see.' Why on earth did he think I should lie about that?"

"Maybe all policemen are skeptical. It's part of their training. Like solicitors." I kissed his cheek.

"Yes, probably so. But you know, darling, it's totally absurd, yet I had the distinct feeling that the sergeant believes I may have arrived early, lured Julian into the tower, and shoved him off!"

5

James stayed the night with me at the Dolphin, an ancient and lovely inn where I had taken a room for the duration of the festival. The next morning, we were finishing a late breakfast when Bettina unexpectedly came into the dining room.

I had called in a press release earlier that morning, simply stating that Mrs. Kingsley was not available for interviews but that the festival would go on despite her husband's tragic death. The unspoken message was that the vultures might badger the police if they had further questions.

Bettina's gray eyes were solemn, as we gestured her to a chair.

"What is it, Bettina?" James asked, concern in his voice.

"Sergeant Glenn rang up Margot at Southmere this morning. There will be an inquest on Julian's death on Monday. It seems they've called in the C.I.D. because they believe Julian may have been pushed to his death. They are treating the case as a probable homicide."

James nodded. "I certainly sensed that last night from the extensive questioning, didn't you?"

Again I saw the look of fear in Bettina's eyes that I had first noticed when we were told that something had happened to Julian. "I did wonder, of course, but I hoped—" She stopped uncertainly.

I finished the thought for her. "That it would be regarded as an accident?"

"Yes."

"Why do the police reject that theory?"

"According to Margot, the sergeant said they've looked over the terrace of the tower in the daylight and found it unlikely that Julian could fall from that spot by accident, even though he had taken a good deal of cocaine."

I said, "The sergeant asked last evening if Julian used drugs but I knew nothing about it."

"Yes, I never told you, Jane. The preliminary tests on the body made the police suspicious. Poor Uncle Julian. It had become a real problem for him. It started as only a social thing, but recently he had become awfully dependent on it. He didn't want anyone at the festival to know."

"Did Margot know?"

"Oh, certainly. In fact, I believe she hinted to the sergeant last evening that this was the cause of her quarrel with Julian."

I didn't quite see Margot as the loving wife concerned over her husband's health, but if Julian's drug habit caused her inconvenience, then she might indeed have quarreled with him about it.

Bettina went on. "What I wanted to ask you two is this. I have masses of things to be seen to. When you come to Southmere today, will you look over the scene at the tower? You might think of a way in which it—er—could have happened. There's a torch just inside the door of the tower. You'll need that to go up the stairs."

We agreed and each gave her a comforting kiss as she sped away. It was, after all, opening night at the festival, and as business manager—or administrator, as the job is often called in England—Bettina was under considerable pressure, even without the distress of her uncle's death. I felt guilty at not being on the job, but Bettina had insisted I spend the day with James.

At least, I thought, Margot was right about one thing. Julian would certainly have wanted the festival to go on. Cancelling at this date would have been a disaster for everybody.

Presently, wearing warm pants and sweaters against the brisk October day, James and I set out on a walk through the picture-postcard town of Burling. James remembered visiting the town once as a child with his parents but had only a vague recollection of a stone tower and some cannon.

I smiled. "Just what a little boy would remember."

We climbed the narrow cobblestone street with its ancient houses, past Lamb House, where the writers Henry James, and later, E. F. Benson, had lived, and on to the fine parish church which dates from Norman times. Beyond the church stood the great tower— much larger than the one at Southmere—with its three-quarter-rounds at the corners, and the gun garden which James remembered.

The town of Burling stands on a hill which rises sharply from the marshes and clings to the top of a sheer cliff on the side facing the sea. In the Middle Ages, when Burling was one of the Cinque Ports, the sea came up to the foot of the cliffs and had begun to eat away large chunks of the town. Then, in the sixteenth century, the pattern reversed. The rivers silted up, the sea receded, and now it lay some miles away, beyond flat marshland. Two small rivers, drifting slowly across the marsh, looked too feeble to pose a threat, but the locals knew that the smuggling which had always formed a part of the town's life was still going on.

As we stood gazing out toward the distant sea, I heard a throaty "hello" and saw Ilena strolling arm in arm with Dmitri Mikos, her stage lover in the opera. Both were warmly dressed, their singers' throats carefully wrapped against the cold.

Last evening, when Ilena sang the aria that passionately proclaims her devotion to the free life, I had wondered if Ilena herself was thinking of putting the motto of *sempre libera* into practice. Ever since the rehearsals began, Dmitri Mikos had wasted no time putting a move on her and she seemed to me to be putting up little protest.

Now, when I had introduced James to the two singers, I said to Ilena, "You're staying over?" Since *Traviata* did not open until Tuesday evening, some of the cast had gone back to London for the weekend.

Ilena shrugged, her dark eyes openly checking out James and deciding he was attractive enough to merit a ravishing smile. "Raymond likes the Dolphin, so we'll stay on."

Dmitri's handsome face looked brooding. "It is too much trouble to go back to London for such short time."

It looked as if Burling had greater attractions for Dmitri at the moment than London could offer, but I blandly murmured, "Yes, of course."

Ilena looked vaguely over her shoulder. "Raymond is doing the 'jog.' So energetic."

And as if she had produced him out of the air, we heard the soft pounding of Reeboks on the stone walk and Ilena's husband jogged past in his designer sweats, waving joyously to all of us, white teeth gleaming through the beard.

At a little gust of wind, Ilena nestled against Dmitri as if for warmth, and we left them standing silently together in the gun garden.

James and I meandered on through the tiny town, admiring the beautifully preserved buildings and looking in shop windows. At an antique shop where I had seen an onyx paperweight that I thought James might like for his desk, I lured him in, casually calling it to his attention and noting that he seemed to admire it. Never too early for gift planning.

Meanwhile, James was studying a tray of rings. "Look, darling, this one's rather charming, don't you think?"

He held out a ring with a garnet circled in pearls, in a gold filigree setting. I loved it, and it looked marvelous on the small finger of my right hand.

The lady of the shop swam forward. "It's lovely, isn't it?" she beamed.

We tried other rings but continually came back to the garnet. At last, James discussed price and the arrangements for having it reduced in size. While measuring my finger on the graduated sizer, she surprised me by asking, "Did your friend find her ring to be satisfactory?"

Then I remembered that on an earlier visit to the shop, I had met Margot coming out, carrying a small parcel.

"Oh, hello, Jane," she had tossed over her shoulder. "I must dash."

"Yes, do," I had managed to fling back at her, hoping she would understand that the last thing I wanted was to detain her, but Margot was no doubt too self-centered to notice.

I had seen Margot wearing an obviously old ring—a

sapphire with diamonds in an intricate setting—and supposed it was one of the Kingsley family heirlooms. Now I wondered if she had simply followed a whim and bought it herself at this shop. She certainly had enough money to buy whatever she liked. Would it rather spoil the fun to have that much money? Here I was, feeling deliciously guilty at James spending so much for my ring. While his legal practice was flourishing, this was still rather a lot for our present means and therefore much more exciting than if we could buy a ring like this every day in the week.

As we left the shop, I protested mildly and was rewarded with one of those looks from James's blue eyes which made me hear the music of the spheres.

"It's not an occasion," I said weakly.

"It's been almost a year, love. We'll call it a pre-anniversary, shall we? Now, let's run over to Southmere and check out the tower for Bettina!"

At Southmere, I walked with James up the hill from the parking area toward the heavy wooden door of the tower. Twenty feet to the right of the entrance we saw brownish splotches on the stone walk. Of course, I thought, there would have been blood which we hadn't seen in the dark the evening before.

I looked at James and saw the same distress on his face that I felt. He shook his head. "You know, darling, if this was murder, as the police seem to think, there must have been a powerful motive to induce someone to push a man to that kind of death."

James pressed hard on the massive door, expecting resistance, but it opened quite readily and with no sound.

Finding the torch inside the entrance, James played its light over the ground floor of the tower, with its repository of ancient bicycles, bits of furniture, and other abandoned objects. "Nothing much here," he said.

As we started up the stone stairs at our left, some light was still visible from the open door below, but as the stairs began to turn and twist, I remembered from my previous visit to the tower with Bettina that there was no light except from the beam of the torch. I had never outgrown a childish terror of dark and enclosed places but I had no intention of giving way, and I plodded sturdily along after James until we reached the first landing. This opened out into a room much like the ground floor, except that it was empty, with four narrow apertures allowing some dim light to penetrate the gloom.

"Marvelous place for a boy—having one's own private tower!"

As we continued up the dark circling steps, I breathed deeply, ignoring my feelings of suffocation. On the second landing, we stepped past an empty room like the one below and went to our right, through the opening onto the small balcony from which Julian had evidently fallen to his death.

Directly ahead, across rolling woodland, the town of Burling perched on its sharply rising promontory. To our left stood the handsome stone buildings and gardens of Southmere, and to our right stretched the line of low wooded hills on one of which the tower had been built.

The little balcony on which we stood was perhaps ten feet by four, surrounded by a solid stone balustrade at least three feet high. We leaned over the wall together and looked down at the spot where Julian had fallen.

James frowned. "Must be close on to forty feet. Poor devil! He must have cried out as he went over.

Wouldn't someone have heard him? Margot told the sergeant there were always people about."

"Not at that hour." I repressed a retort about Margot's exaggerations. "Did you see anyone when you arrived?"

James looked slightly startled. "No, as a matter of fact, the place was quite deserted."

"Exactly."

I gave him a moment to think that one through, then pointed to the traces of dry powder scattered over the stones of the terrace, remarking that the police seemed to have done their work. "But they must not have found anything," I added, "or they would have someone in custody by now."

"On the other hand, love, think of the number of people who have come up to the tower recently. Probably half a dozen of those connected with the festival have made the tour up here, just as you did. Everyone would lean over this parapet and leave prints all over the place."

"At least you're in the clear, James. You've never been here before."

James smiled wryly. "They'd merely say I wore gloves."

"If only it could have been an accident." I leaned against the balustrade, vainly trying to believe that Julian could have toppled over. "He had used a heavy dose of cocaine. Could he have been terribly dizzy and simply fallen?"

"If anyone's tried for his murder, that will certainly be a major argument for the defense. Frankly, I think it's unlikely he could fall that way, but anything's possible."

"The thing is, *why* did he come all the way up here? If he planned to meet someone at the tower, surely they would transact their business on the ground floor?''

James shook his head. "The police must be asking themselves the same question. I'm afraid we haven't found much here to help Bettina."

As we turned to go, we heard a "Hi, there!" from below and saw the black curly head of Anton Szabo, his arm waving a casual hello. When we reached the ground, we found Anton staring down at the blood-stains on the stone walk.

"Jesus! Look at that!" Anton shook his head in disgust. "Kingsley really must've flipped. He was a great guy but he couldn't get off the stuff. I tried to warn him. Even the blonde bitch raised hell about it."

Then he looked at James. "Oh, shit! Sorry, I guess she's a pal of yours."

James said, "Never mind. So you think it was an accident, do you?"

"Sure, what else?"

"The police seem to think it was murder."

"No kidding?" Anton grinned. "So what were you doing up there? Visiting the scene of the crime?"

I sidestepped his question by steering him to the one subject which I knew would absorb his attention. "Is everything all set for tonight's opening, Anton?"

As the three of us strolled down the hill toward the gardens, Anton engaged in a litany of complaints about everyone from the technicians to the principal singers. His chief target of the moment was Russell Ames, the conductor.

"Every time I need a really dramatic effect, Ames says the singers can't do it that way, or it won't work with the orchestra."

"Who gives a damn about the music?" I said sweetly.

James choked, but Anton looked only mildly puzzled. "Yeah, sure the music's important, but Christ, you've got to stop thinking like everybody else, if you know what I mean. Ames is a good musician, I'll give him that. But maybe next year we'll look for somebody else—"

I stopped and stared at Anton. "Next year?" Insensitive as Anton was, it surprised me that he had apparently given no thought to whether the festival would go on after Julian's death.

Now his dark eyes blinked. "Oh, I see what you mean. But Julian wasn't really on the artistic side. Sure, he and Ames and I worked together on everything, but Julian was the money man."

James said, "And will the money be available again next year?"

Anton shrugged. "There was talk of some syndicate popping with a load of cash. Then there's the niece—Bettina. She's gung-ho for the project, and she'll probably come in for a wad from uncle."

I saw no reason to confide in Anton that Bettina was probably cut off with the proverbial shilling. "What about Margot?" I asked.

James nodded. "She might want to continue the festival in memory of her husband."

I stole a glance to see if he was serious. He was serious. Oh, well. I expected a howl of derision from Anton and was surprised to hear him agree with James. "Yes, Margot might do that. Even though she doesn't know shit about opera—" Now the old sneering tone was back.

"The problem is," I said, "that a festival like this needs an absolutely dedicated man like Julian to head it up."

Anton looked solemn, but a trace of smugness crossed his face. "Yeah, poor old Julian. He did a great job."

As we reached the parking area, Anton flipped his hand in farewell and headed for the stage door.

I smiled. "It looks as if Anton is ready to take over the reins."

James raised an eyebrow. "Perhaps he disposed of Julian in order to become his successor?"

"The only trouble with that theory is that he already had Julian eating out of his hand. Julian was totally opinionated with most people, but Anton could do no wrong. Anton already was, in effect, the artistic director of the festival."

6

During the half-hour or so before curtain that evening, I was on duty in the foyer, receiving the London critics, many of whom I knew by sight, and welcoming those from other areas who presented themselves at the press desk. James stood by, smiling and looking very dear, in my eyes, in black tie and tails. Following the custom at Glyndebourne, everyone was in evening dress. The special feel of an opening night was in the air, and when the crowded foyer finally emptied and the first notes of the prologue sounded from the orchestra, we slipped quickly into our seats at the back of the stalls.

Benjamin Britten's *The Turn of the Screw* was a fine choice for performance at a small and intimate theater like Southmere. With its cast of six singers, accompanied by a chamber group of thirteen musicians, this little gem of an opera dramatizes the familiar story by Henry James of the Victorian governess whose young charges are haunted by the ghosts of their former governess and a sinister manservant.

For this production Anton Szabo had surprised me by showing how good a designer he could be when he stopped being artsy. After the prologue, the curtain opened to reveal in stage center the porch of the country house where the children, Miles and Flora, eagerly await the arrival of the new governess. With a few deft touches, Anton's house front suggested elegance, while a shimmer of trees in the distance sheltered the tower where the ghost of Peter Quint would first appear. The scene changes were controlled with lighting, with the charmingly furnished schoolroom at stage right, while stage left, when lit, revealed the lake, on the far side of which the governess first sees the figure of Miss Jessel.

The ghostly appearances were brilliantly handled. Peter Quint would appear to the governess, staring at her with evil arrogance, then simply vanish, giving the audience as well as the governess a *frisson* of terror.

Anton's direction carefully paced the alternating scenes of happy normalcy and increasing eeriness as the governess becomes aware that the children are under the spell of the ghost figures. With Russell Ames conducting the difficult and sometimes obscure music with sensitivity, the production was decidedly a success.

At the interval between the two acts, when we mingled with the crowds in the foyer, we heard exclamations of pleasure. Bettina was there, chatting with various VIPs and receiving murmured condolences on the death of her uncle. Julian's death was of course a prime topic of conversation, the consensus being that it must somehow have been an accident. Anything else was unthinkable.

Margot remained in seclusion at the main house, fifty yards or so from the theater at Southmere. Probably relieved not to have to attend the performance, I thought. But where was Simon, Bettina's husband? When I asked her, she said he had been called away on business that morning and wasn't sure he could make it back for the opening.

As we moved away, I said to James, "I wonder where Simon was off to?"

On our way to visit the tower that morning, we had seen a lorry coming out of the drive from Southmere onto the main road and noticed Simon sitting beside the driver, talking earnestly. The side of the truck was labeled City Freight Services, Ltd., the name of the firm with which Simon had some connection, and James had remarked that the red hair and beard of the driver reminded him of someone.

"He looks a bit like the Irish chap the police found last night at the tower after Kingsley was killed—Mick Corcoran, wasn't it? Said he had an appointment with Kingsley. I trust he'll turn out to be a prime suspect. I don't fancy the role for myself!"

I had laughed. "Don't worry, darling. You hadn't seen Margot for three or four years. They could hardly imagine the old flame was still burning after that length of time."

To my surprise, I had seen James flinch slightly. Oh, well, I had thought, I must stop being flippant about it. It's probably still a painful memory for him.

Now, back in the theater for the final act of the opera, I forgot everything else, as Henry James's tale of the corruption of innocence moved toward its conclusion. When the governess at last persuades little Miles to repudiate the evil Quint, only to have the boy die in her arms, there was that flattering moment of hushed silence after the last note of music and before the storm of applause, which signals a moving performance. I knew the reviews would be good, and I couldn't help being glad that this production, and not the controversial *Traviata,* was the season opener.

Backstage, the usual high spirits were somewhat

subdued in deference to Julian's death. None of the six singers in this production had been present the night before, having all gone back to London after their dress rehearsal the preceding Thursday, and no one had been able to answer their shocked questions about Julian. The police hadn't been heard from all day, and these six were at least happy to be clear of suspicion. They wouldn't be needed again until the next performance of *Turn* four days later, as Julian had scheduled the two operas to provide three or four days' rest for the singers.

Russell Ames warmly congratulated his cast, and even Anton Szabo managed a few words of praise. I was amused to see that the members of the *Traviata* cast who were still around had come backstage. Ilena came in on Raymond's arm, followed by Dmitri Mikos and Riccardo Palma. As they offered their gushing compliments, I suppressed a cynical smile. Even when they were perfectly sincere, singers congratulating other singers always managed to sound phony to me.

Now Raymond turned his gleaming teeth in my direction. "You know, Jane, they've got the story all wrong. There aren't any ghosts in *The Turn of the Screw*. It's all in the mind of the governess. She was just a frustrated spinster who was in love with the children's guardian and imagined the whole thing."

I sighed. "Raymond, dear, I've heard that Freudian interpretation and it's terribly ingenious. There's only one thing wrong with it: Henry James *said* he was writing a ghost story. He loved them and wrote dozens of them and this was one of his favorites."

Raymond grinned at me as delightedly as if I had agreed with him. Nodding sagely, he said, "Maybe the old boy didn't realize what he was doing."

I groaned and decided to abandon literary criticism

in favor of food. "Look, Raymond, some of us are going to Mario's. Why don't you and Ilena come along?"

A town as small as Burling did not bristle with late-hours restaurants, but we had arranged with Mario to receive a sizable group that evening. Accordingly, by half-past ten I found myself squeezed between James and Bettina at a round table crowded with a dozen refugees from the opera, all wolfing down pasta and red wine.

At Bettina's right, Russell Ames gazed at her through his black-rimmed glasses, trying to look casual but with adoration oozing from every pore, while Bettina, like the girl in the Virgin Spring, saw nothing but friendliness. At thirty-three, Russell was well on the way to a promising career. Having been the protégé of a well-known conductor, he got off to a good start, making the usual rounds of the smaller European orchestras and opera houses, then moving up on the scale to occasional assignments in the big houses. When I did the promo, I was able to list appearances for him in Rome, Paris, and Salzburg, as well as some good items forthcoming. A serious conductor, talented and hard-working, his careful preparation of scores earned him the respect of the musicians he worked with.

Bettina had told me, with sorrow in her great eyes, that Russell had been in love with a mezzo from Sweden who had left him for a bassoon player. "Poor Russell, he's so unhappy," Bettina had said. I could have told her that if she herself hadn't been married to Simon, Russell's broken heart would have mended in a hurry, but she wouldn't have believed me, nor would it have helped Russell if she had. No one was more true blue than Bettina.

Looking around the table, I saw Ilena between Dmitri and Raymond, looking rather sulky, I thought, but Raymond seemed to notice nothing, beaming away at both of them equally. Riccardo Palma had brought along an attractive young woman from the chorus with whom he seemed to be on exceedingly friendly terms. Anton Szabo wasn't there, having declined the invitation with a graceless "Thanks, no," as he hurried off backstage.

As the wine bottles circulated, things warmed up, and by the time the party broke up, everyone was feeling festive. That's when Bettina, as we saw her to her car, dropped a minor bombshell. She was saying good night when she exclaimed, "Oh, gosh, I nearly forgot. Margot is having Julian's solicitor in at eleven tomorrow to read Julian's will and she wants James to be there, sort of for legal advice, I expect. Can you come?"

I said to James, "Of course, darling, go ahead."

James frowned, then put his arm around my shoulder. "Yes, all right. Please tell Margot we'll both be there."

Over my faint objections, James marched me firmly off to Southmere the following morning for the reading of Julian Kingsley's will. I was mildly surprised that Julian had gone to a local solicitor in the tiny town of Burling for his will, until I learned that John Kemp was a boyhood friend whom Julian had liked and trusted.

Old Alfred greeted us at the door, muttering about the police badgering him. "I *told* them I saw no one leave through the stage door before Mr. Julian met with his accident." He shook his head sadly as we offered condolences. I refrained from pointing out that anyone could have slipped out of the theater by an-

43

other exit. Old Alfred evidently found comfort in regarding his master's death as an accident, not a murder.

Now, in the drawing room at Southmere, we found Margot on a small sofa by the fire, with Simon at her side. Bettina introduced John Kemp, and we joined the circle, while Kemp took out his papers and put on a pair of rimless glasses. As I knew very well from being married to one, solicitors don't normally make house calls on a Sunday morning, but when you're dealing with the Kingsley millions, it's another matter.

Margot was looking devastating as usual in tight pants and a knit top, her heavy blonde hair swinging as she threw her head back against the cushion. "So let's have it, John. Has the poor widow been left a mite or two?"

John Kemp's face remained impassive. "I believe you'll find everything quite in order, Margot. Julian came to me shortly after his marriage to you nearly three years ago and a document was drawn at that time, according to his wishes. Then, a year or so later, after the marriage of Bettina and Simon, Julian made a new will, and that is the document that we have before us."

I stole a glance at Bettina, who nodded serenely, and then at Simon, who looked equally unconcerned. They both knew that Julian had threatened to cut Bettina out if she married Simon, but I for one had wondered if he had really done it. Now it looked as if he had.

Skipping the legal language, and the bequests to various servants and some distant cousins, the will designated a large sum to continue the support of the Southmere Opera Festival, named the sum of five thousand pounds to Bettina Harcourt Barnes "for her personal use," and left the bulk of the estate to Margot Kingsley.

I remembered that Bettina's mother, the sister of Julian Kingsley, had inherited a large sum on the death of their father, but most of the money had been squandered by a series of fortune-hunting husbands, leaving Bettina with only a small income.

The only surprise in Julian's will was a bequest to one Veeda Riley, at 20 Gorston Road, London, for the sum of ten thousand pounds.

"Who on earth is Veeda Riley?" Bettina asked, and was greeted with frozen silence. Kemp's eyes remained fixed on his papers. Simon gazed discreetly into the fire. I glanced at James and saw his eyes flicker toward Margot and away again.

Then Margot spoke, her voice harsh. "I'll tell you who Veeda Riley is. She's that tart Julian used to see. I hope he got his money's worth."

John Kemp stirred. "I believe she was an old friend, Margot, nothing more."

Margot shrugged. "Well, it doesn't matter now, does it? Let's have the sherry, Bettina."

As we stood about, sipping the ritual sherry, I reflected that if Margot was right and the mysterious Veeda Riley had been Julian's mistress, it would mean that the relationship had continued after his marriage to Margot, since the current will had been drawn more than a year afterward. More puzzling was my feeling that everyone in the room but Bettina had known who Veeda Riley was—even James. But how could James know anything about Julian Kingsley's private life? I must be imagining things.

Margot hung about James, asking what seemed to me inane questions and declaring she would ring him if she needed legal advice.

As we drove back to our hotel in Burling, I casually

asked James if he had ever heard of Veeda Riley and saw a slight flush of embarrassment tinge his cheek.

"Oh, I may have heard the name," he said, with an unconvincing attempt at airiness. What on earth was going on? I said nothing more, but only a few hours later, when I had the answer to my question, it came with a shock I'll not soon forget.

7

That afternoon James and I drove back to London, where I would stay over and go back to Burling the next day. On the drive we had avoided the whole subject of Margot and company, but now, as we munched a snack in the kitchen of our flat, I remarked that Simon had behaved quite decently at the reading of the will. "He said not a word about Julian's obvious gibe in leaving Bettina's money 'for her personal use,' to say nothing of five thousand pounds being a paltry sum for Julian to leave his beloved niece."

"I expect Simon was prepared for that, since Kingsley had threatened to cut her off if she married Simon. What puzzles me, Jane, is that Simon and Bettina seemed to be on fairly good terms with her uncle—staying at the house, working on the festival, and so on. It's true Riccardo heard Julian and Simon quarreling one day, but that may have been over something quite trivial. Why would Kingsley have had them at Southmere at all if he disliked Simon so much?"

"I more or less asked Bettina that myself when I first went down to Burling two weeks ago. She said that when Simon married her without any prospect of her uncle's money, Julian thawed a bit toward him. The two of them seemed to operate on a basis of mutual toleration, and of course I could see that Julian actually adored Bettina and didn't want to be cut off from her. I suspect that in the course of time he might have relented about the money. After all, no one expected him to die at the age of forty-eight.''

''Poor chap.'' I saw the compassion in James's blue eyes and kissed the top of his head as I went for the coffee pot to pour our refills.

Then we reverted to the topic which currently absorbed us more than *l'affaire* Kingsley. James was representing a young man who had been accused of a robbery during which a man was shot and wounded.

It had happened four days earlier, on the Wednesday evening, in Theobald's Road, not far from our flat, at a gunsmith shop. At about two o'clock in the morning, two men had broken into the shop and were rapidly filling a sack with handguns and ammunition when the proprietor, Thomas Wilkins, who lived upstairs, heard them and rang up the police. Then, instead of waiting for the police to arrive, he foolishly started down the stairs, carrying a revolver, and called out to the men to drop their loot. He fired a warning shot, hoping to frighten them off, but one of the robbers, no doubt believing his life to be in danger, fired two shots, one of which struck Wilkins in the chest. The owner's wife and twelve-year-old son then rushed down to the landing of the stairs and caught a glimpse of the two men as they dropped their sack and fled to a waiting car. Later, it was learned that two handguns were missing from the shop.

When the police arrived minutes later, Wilkins lay bleeding on the stairs, protesting that he only meant to frighten the men away. The wife had meanwhile called for an ambulance and the wounded man was taken to the hospital.

The distraught Mrs. Wilkins could give no description of the men, except that they were wearing ski masks. Her son added that the men wore sneakers and that one was taller than the other. They had heard one of the men shout some sort of obscenity at the other, but neither could recall the precise words used. The same voice had called out, "Let's go!" just before the men ran from the shop.

The police, who had found one ski mask on the pavement near the front of the shop, searched the area and stopped a car halfway up the hill on Rosebery Avenue, a quarter of a mile away, driven by a man in his early twenties, accompanied by another man, aged twenty-eight. Both men wore sneakers, dark pullovers, and gloves, and one was distinctly taller than the other. No handguns were found in the car or on their persons.

The two men were taken in for questioning. By that time Wilkins was known to be in critical condition, and when it was learned from the computer that both men had prior convictions for burglary and had served prison terms, the two were held at the police station.

James's client was the younger and taller of the two men—Dan Hawks, age twenty-two, a resident of Islington, not far from the statue of the Angel, the familiar landmark for that area of London. Hawks was not the wide-eyed innocent one might like for a client. He was surly and unprepossessing but adamant that he and his chum "never shot nobody."

"We don't work with no firearms," he had told James over and over, and James was inclined to believe him innocent, in part because armed robberies are not all that common in Great Britain, but even more because at the time the police stopped his car, Hawks was driving *slowly* along the road.

"Nobody who's just committed a shooting is going to be found ten to fifteen minutes later no farther away than Rosebery Avenue, cruising along at low speed," James had said from the beginning.

At the magistrate's court the next day, he had tried to have the charges dropped, but the magistrate, citing Hawks's prior convictions for burglary, had refused. When bail was set, Hawks's mother had signed the bond so that her son could be released until the time of the trial.

The case had come to James in a roundabout fashion. Hawks was disillusioned with his former solicitor, who had been provided through legal aid. A neighbor had recommended one of James's partners, who seldom handled criminal proceedings and passed it along to James. As the youngest member of the firm of which his father had been the senior partner before his death, James found himself doing whatever criminal practice came along, finding it to be more interesting than he had expected.

Now I asked, "What does Hawks say about the police theory that he and his chum must have been familiar with Wilkins's shop because they live nearby in Islington?" Anyone driving toward the West End of London from Islington might well take the route from Rosebery Avenue along Theobald's Road, where Wilkins's shop is located, then follow the jog down to Holborn High Street, which is one-way going west. On the return trip, he would follow Theobald's Road straight through, as it goes one-way east.

"He admits to driving along Theobald's Road many times but says he took no notice of the gunsmith shop, not being on the lookout for firearms. He says he never stops at the shops there as it's too hard to find a spot to park."

"How well we know that!" I regularly shopped at the greengrocer next to Wilkins's place, as well as at other shops along Theobald's Road, and found it easier to walk from our flat than to look for a parking spot.

"So he claims he's never been in Wilkins's shop at all?"

"Exactly."

Just then the buzzer sounded from the security entrance to our flat, an innovation for our building, which dated from the middle of the last century.

When I lifted the phone, a voice said, "Mr. James Hall, please. We are police officers."

"Yes, of course." I released the outer door and presently we heard the ring at our door. James peered through the peephole, then turned the double locks to admit two officers in plainclothes.

A stocky man of medium height held out his ID. "I am Detective Chief Inspector Collier of the East Sussex Constabulary. This is Detective Sergeant Morton of the Metropolitan Police. We should like to ask you a few questions if we may."

Assuming that their visit concerned Dan Hawks or another of James's cases, I smiled cordially and invited the officers to be seated, but the chief inspector merely glanced around the flat and spoke to James. "Is anyone else on the premises?"

"No, no one."

Then he looked at me and back at James. "We'd like to have a word with you in private, Mr. Hall."

I said, "Of course," and started for the kitchen. I heard James say, "Is this concerning the Hawks case, then?"

51

"Hawks? No, sir. We are investigating the homicide of Mr. Julian Kingsley."

James said, "Oh, I see. Well then, we may as well have my wife present. She was there at Southmere at the time."

I sat down and gestured for the officers to take chairs, but again Chief Inspector Collier made no response, saying to James, "You might prefer to come down to the station, sir, to answer a few questions."

James stared at him, then spoke sharply. "No, Chief Inspector, whatever you have to say may be said in the presence of my wife."

Collier shrugged. "Very well." At last he sat down, and the sergeant did likewise, holding his notebook at the ready.

Collier cleared his throat. "Mr. Hall, you do not have to say anything unless you wish to do so, but anything you do say may be put into writing and given in evidence."

James looked startled. "Good grief, are you cautioning me? I'm a solicitor, you know. This hardly seems necessary."

Collier's tone was icy. "I am aware of your profession, sir. You must therefore understand the necessity for the caution. Now, Mr. Hall, in the course of our investigation, we have looked for any persons connected with Mr. Kingsley or his wife who might have a reason for wishing to put Mr. Kingsley out of the way. When it was learned that you had been at one time, shall we say, a close friend of Mrs. Kingsley, your picture was shown to the doorman at the Kingsley flat in Mayfair. This person has confirmed that you have visited the flat on at least two occasions in recent weeks when Mrs. Kingsley was present and when Mr. Julian was in residence at Southmere. Do you agree that this information is correct?"

"Yes, Chief Inspector, that is correct."

I felt a lump of pain in the middle of my chest, but I kept my eyes lowered and gave no sign of surprise.

I heard James's voice go on. "Mrs. Kingsley had requested that I call on her to discuss legal problems. You understand, I am sure, that the nature of our discussions is privileged. Since Mrs. Kingsley, as my client, requested absolute secrecy, I was unable to inform anyone, even my wife, of these visits."

Collier's eyebrow rose an insulting fraction. "Of course, sir. And did you at any time during these visits renew a more intimate personal relation with Mrs. Kingsley?"

"No, certainly not. Our discussions were entirely professional. Surely Mrs. Kingsley was asked the same question?"

Something very close to a smirk appeared on Collier's face. "Yes, sir, she was. She did not absolutely assert that the interviews were totally impersonal."

"Well, I can assure you that they were."

Now Collier shifted ground. "As for the evening of Friday last, you have stated that you arrived at the Sussex residence of the Kingsleys, called Southmere, at approximately seven o'clock?"

"I believe it was somewhat after seven."

Then they went over again and again the story of James finding Julian Kingsley on the walk by the tower and the subsequent events of that evening.

At last, the officers took their leave, with Collier declaring as his parting shot that they would be talking with James again in the near future.

I was furious. "They can't be serious, darling," I fumed. "It's too ridiculous."

Now that I had had time to absorb the shock of learning that James had in fact seen Margot in recent weeks, I saw that he was in no way to blame. I could easily believe that James might be taken in by Margot's dramatics and feel sorry for her, as he had at Southmere the evening I saw her hanging about his neck, but surely he wouldn't have gone to her flat and made love to her, to say nothing of murdering Julian.

But what was Margot up to, letting the police think what they obviously did? With her ego, she evidently had to appear irresistible to all men, whatever the consequences.

Now James was holding both my hands. "I'm so sorry about all this, darling. You don't believe—?"

I looked into those clear blue eyes. "No, I don't. I know you, James, and if you had fallen for Margot again, I would have known at once that something was wrong, and when I asked you, you would have told me the truth. But why on earth did Margot imply to the police what she did?"

I could see James struggling with that one. "I don't know. But I'll tell you the whole story now, Jane. Margot first rang me up at the office about three weeks ago, shortly before you went down to Southmere, and asked me to come to her place for a consultation. Of course I suggested that she consult another solicitor, but she insisted that it must be someone she knew and trusted, as the matter was confidential. When I arrived, she told me she was terribly worried about her husband, that he was going rather heavily into cocaine, and she had seen some rather shady characters hanging about who might be luring him into trouble.

"I said that surely Kingsley's drug use was a matter for a doctor, not a solicitor. As for the other, perhaps a private investigator could check out his associates if she felt seriously concerned. She said that was exactly what she wanted but had no idea where to look. I recommended the firm that we use on occasion, she thanked me, offered me a fee which I declined, and I left."

"No personal conversation at all?" I couldn't see Margot sticking to business so admirably.

James smiled faintly. "Of course we spoke briefly of mutual acquaintances from the past. Then she said she knew you were going down to Southmere and that she looked forward to meeting you and asked if I would be coming down. I told her our plans for this weekend, that sort of thing. Then she insisted that I tell no one she had spoken with me."

Holding her fire, I thought.

"It was some time in the following week that Margot rang me again, sounding distressed. I went to her place straight from the office. This time she told me she had learned that Kingsley was still seeing a woman named Veeda Riley, an old flame from before their marriage. She tried to hold up but there were tears, I'm afraid, and I offered what comfort I could."

Poor James. Sir Galahad coping with the *belle dame sans merci*. "Of course, dear," I murmured.

"Well, then, we talked at some length about possible divorce proceedings, but in the end she said she really cared for her husband and didn't want to end the marriage. She seemed to feel better for having talked it out with someone. By this time, of course, you were at Southmere, Jane, and Margot said you were as beautiful and charming as I had told her you were."

No doubt disappointed I wasn't a total frump, I thought.

"Actually, that's more or less what happened on both occasions when I saw Margot. I suppose she might have regarded her emotional outburst on the second visit as 'personal' rather than professional, and perhaps that's why she failed to assure the police on that score."

Oh, of course, I thought. But I saw that the seeds of doubt about Margot were well and truly sown and no cynical comment from me was needed to make James wary of her from here on.

8

The next morning, I walked with James as far as Theobald's Road, where he went on to his office in Grays Inn, one of London's historic Inns of Court. One of the advantages of our living in unfashionable Bloomsbury was that James did not have to battle traffic morning and evening. Besides, we both loved the area where James had always lived and where I had first come to live in London three years earlier.

Now, with my shopping bag over my arm—no London housewife would be caught dead without one—I stopped at the bakery for a few items and went on to the greengrocer's for some fruit, to keep James supplied while I was away for the week. I couldn't help looking with some curiosity at Wilkins's shop as I passed, where the stout Mrs. Wilkins, her brown hair straggling over her reddish face, could be seen at the counter serving a customer.

"Nothing for it but to carry on," I heard her say as I went past the door. "He'll be in hospital for some time, the doctors say." I stifled the impulse to step in and offer my condolences, for it scarcely seemed appropriate from the wife of the solicitor who was representing one of the men accused of shooting the woman's husband.

At the shop next door, the shooting was still a prime topic. Asking if I had heard the news, the young woman helping me didn't wait for my answer before launching into a lurid account of poor Mr. Wilkins lying in pools of blood on his own stairs. "And we in bed upstairs here, not knowing nothing about it till we hear the police and all the commotion."

"Didn't you hear the gunshots?" I asked.

"Something woke me what sounded like popping noises but I never thought it was bullets, now, would I?"

I heard the clatter of a skateboard and a boy I soon learned was Tommy Wilkins bumped his way into the shop.

"Not in school today, Tommy?" his neighbor asked.

A cheeky lad with a likable grin, Tommy did a turn on his skateboard, threatening to topple a display of apples. "No. I was let off coz we have to go talk to the fuzz again."

"What about? Haven't you told 'em everything already?"

"Right, but more ones have to hear it over again. All I saw was the ski masks and their sneakers, and I heard the one hollering at the other one as he shot at me dad, but I don't know the words. Sounded like 'bloody shit' but I can't be sure."

And helping himself to an apple, Tommy rolled out of the shop and down the pavement of Theobald's Road.

Back at the flat, I stashed the food away and nipped down to where the car was parked a few doors down on our street, clutching my trusty *A to Z,* the London street guide without which life in the city would come to a dead halt. Still steaming at the idea that James could be suspected of murder, I had decided to take some action, whether it did any good or not. It seemed to me that if somebody had actually shoved Julian Kingsley off the tower, it might well be one of the shady characters Margot had told James she was worried about. I wondered if in fact she had employed the investigator James had recommended.

Meanwhile, there was one connection I could follow up. I had looked up 20 Gorston Road, the address of Veeda Riley, the woman to whom Julian had left a chunk of money in his will. She might know something about Julian's associates the rest of us didn't know. I had a few hours before returning to Southmere. What better than to do some sleuthing on my own?

I drove up to the Euston Road, went west through Marylebone, and came into Kilburn, a heavily Irish area, where the police sometimes searched for hide-outs after an IRA bombing. Gorston Road, when I found it, was a street like hundreds of others in London, with its endless row of joined houses of dingy brick, three stories high, each divided into flats. In tonier areas, fresh paint and brightly colored front doors, together with strategically placed plantings, induced a certain charm in the old buildings, but in Gorston Road, only a lace-curtained window here and there put up a feeble protest against the flaking paint and the trash-littered areaways.

Number twenty looked no better than its neighbors. When Veeda Riley gets her ten thousand pounds, I thought, she will probably make a rapid exit from the neighborhood. Scanning the faded names on the door plate, I found her in the top flat and climbed two pairs of dark, uncarpeted stairs. No one answered my ring, and I was about to give up when I heard someone coming up the stairs. A woman with auburn hair came along the landing, looking startled when she saw me.

"Looking for someone, then?" Her voice was husky.

"Ms. Riley?"

"I'm Veeda Riley." Groping in a copious bag for her key, she looked at me curiously.

"I'm Jane Winfield Hall." Sometimes the double name was the easiest way out. "I'd like to talk to you, if you don't mind."

"I don't mind. Come in."

The interior of the flat was something of a surprise. Dark green carpet, gold plush sofa with a marble-topped table graced with magazines and a bowl of artificial but not bad-looking flowers.

Mrs. Riley tossed her coat over a chair and went to a side table, where she poured out two glasses of sherry, handing me one without asking if I wanted it. Half past ten in the morning was a mite early but I'd have taken anything she offered to keep her happy.

Now she sank into a low chair and looked me over. I took a corner of the sofa and looked back. Veeda Riley was probably in her early forties, with deep, violet blue eyes, thickly springing hair with gray showing at the roots where the auburn tint had grown out, and a body that still looked sensational.

"You're not from the police, then? They have some young good lookers like you these days, but you're American, right?"

"Right." I hate exchanges of "Right/Right" but this was no time for quibbles.

"So, what do you want to talk about?"

"About Julian Kingsley."

"He's dead."

"Yes. Did you know he left you some money?"

If I expected a look of pleasure, even triumph, I was

disappointed. The violet eyes gave no sign. The sultry voice was flat. "I know. The lawyer rang me up this morning."

"Were you surprised?"

"No. Julian always told me I would come in for something if anything happened to him."

"You were—er—old friends?"

Now she finally asked the question I had been expecting. "So what is your interest in this?"

I decided that subterfuge would be pointless and described my connection with the Southmere Festival, the events surrounding Julian's death, and the visit from the police the evening before, when James was questioned.

"But what motive would your husband have?"

No use turning back now. I told her about the long affair between James and Margot in the past and indicated, without mentioning James's recent visits to Margot, that the police suspected the relationship had been renewed.

"I know it isn't true. I suppose all wives say that, but if you knew James—"

The violet eyes looked into mine. "Have they asked *her* about it?"

"Yes, and evidently she has not absolutely denied it."

"The bitch!"

For the first time, I saw animation in that masked face. "Your James is a lucky devil, luv. Just you keep him away from her. But what can I do for you?"

"I want to know more about Julian—his past life and so on. I thought you might be able to fill me in, Mrs. Riley."

"Veeda, luv. Call me Veeda. And you?"

"Jane."

"All right, Jane." She kicked off her shoes and

stretched her legs. "Fetch the sherry, there's a luv."

I brought the bottle to the low table between us and filled her empty glass, topping mine. Veeda drank hers off and filled it up again herself.

"Julian and I go back a long way. Sixteen years and more. Before his first wife died. I was managing a music and record shop in the West End in those days. Now I own a small chain—actually four shops around London. So Julian came into the shop one day with a complicated order, and the shop assistant called me out from the office to help."

I was surprised. Somehow I had pictured this languidly sexy woman as the traditional kept mistress, spending her days painting her nails and going to the hairdresser, not as a competent businesswoman.

"God, he was a gorgeous man." The violet eyes were shot with light. "I wasn't too hard to look at myself then. We met a few times for drinks, and then it was off to a hotel. His wife was already ill, poor thing. Died of cancer, you know. He really cared for her in his own way, but Julian wasn't a man to be a faithful husband. It was different for me. I was already married to Riley at the time and this was my first fling. That's the way I thought of it at first, you see, just a fling.

"But as time went on, it grew more serious. It seems as if we couldn't do without seeing each other from time to time. After his wife died, he had other women—he made no secret of that—but he always came back to me. After a while, Riley and I went our separate ways. We're still married—we'd done it up proper at St. Ursula's—and divorce isn't worth the bother, is it, unless one of us wanted to marry again?"

I made no response but simply refilled her glass

when she held it out. I sensed that she was speaking less to me than to herself. Julian's death must have been a shock for her, no matter how cool she wanted to appear.

She went on, as if answering a question I hadn't asked. "No, Julian and I never talked about marriage. I wouldn't have fit in to all that la-di-da at Southmere, and I didn't care for the money. That may sound odd, but it's true. I think that's one reason Julian knew he could trust me. People who grow up with all that wealth always suspect their friends are after something, and usually they are. It's true Julian lent me the money to buy the first shop, but I paid it back, every cent, and I've been on my own ever since. I like it that way."

Now Veeda seemed to remember I was there and favored me with a shrewd smile. "It worked all right for me, too. Being independent, I could have my own friends as I liked, couldn't I now?"

I smiled back. I liked this woman, and I suppose it showed, for she said, "You're all right, Jane. I thought you might be Miss Priss, but I see you're not."

Another gulp of sherry. "So we jogged along for some years, Julian and I. He was always flying about the world going to operas and such, and now and then I'd go along for the holiday. I give my staff top wages and it pays in the end, as I can take off when I like and know they'll keep things going for me. Like to-day—I didn't feel much like going in to work."

"Yes, I understand."

"So, after a time Julian sort of gave up on the other woman and for a long while we were together a good deal and getting on like an old married couple.

"Then he met Her Highness, and that tied it. He was totally besotted with her from the beginning. He told me he had gone to the races one day with a friend

63

and met this stunning young woman—she was twenty-seven and Julian was already forty-four—but she was engaged to the man she was with. Was that your husband, luv?''

"No, it wasn't James. Margot had gone off with someone else before she met Julian.''

"I see. Well, then, apparently Her Highness rang up Julian and they started meeting, and I needn't make a drawing for you to see how things went on from there. He used to ring me up to report on how the romance was going. You'd have thought I was his mum. And when they were going to be married, Julian was as excited as a boy in his teens.

"I admit I felt pretty low for a time. That's when I began with too much of this.'' She poured another sherry as if to illustrate her point.

"I didn't see him for six months after the marriage, and I thought it was all over between us. Then one evening he arrived, looking sort of hangdog and sheepish at the same time, if you know what I mean.''

I found it hard to picture Julian Kingsley looking anything but powerfully in control. Margot must really have got to him.

"He told me she was bitchy to live with and at times he was miserable. You see, his first wife had been one of those quiet types who catered to him in everything. This one was a different proposition altogether. Before they were married, she had been sweet as an angel but that didn't last long. She was bored with life at South-mere, which Julian loved, and hated everything to do with opera. She was always running up to London, which was all right with him if it had made her more content, but she was sulky and bad-tempered a good deal of the time.''

"Did he think of divorce?''

"Oh, he talked about it, especially during the first

year. That was when I began to see what his real problem was. The poor man was still mad about her. He could no more have left her than he could have stopped breathing. Sometimes she would quite suddenly turn affectionate, and then he forgave her everything. At last, he settled in and seemed to accept her for what she was, but he needed to see me from time to time. He said I was his anchor, and I didn't mind. You see, he was the only man I ever really cared for.''

While Veeda poured the last of the sherry into her glass, I asked, "Was Margot seeing other men?"

"No, that's the odd thing. Apparently, she flirted a bit at parties and that, but Julian never once suspected her of carrying on with anyone. That's the one thing he wouldn't have tolerated, I'm sure."

As she spoke, I saw the first signs of the effect of the nearly full bottle of sherry she had downed in a relatively short time. There was no slurring in her speech, but her body slouched and her eyelids blinked more slowly.

I said, "I'm glad Julian left you something in his will. It could make things pleasanter for you, I expect."

The violet eyes stared at the artificial flowers on the table. Then the husky voice murmured, "They'll never let me keep it."

I was startled. "Do you mean the lawyers? Surely, it's legal?"

"No, luv, I mean my—" Abruptly, she struggled to her feet. "Now, then, I mustn't keep you."

It was a neat dismissal, firm but not rude. I thanked her and sped away down the stairs, grateful to have learned something about Julian and Margot, even if it had no bearing on the question of his murder.

As I backed my car, I noticed a dark green lorry

with City Freight Services, Ltd. lettered in white. Simon's firm, I remembered. I looked at the driver but it was not Simon, it was the man with the vivid red hair—Mick Corcoran—whom we had seen in the lorry with Simon and who had had the appointment with Julian on the night of his death.

9

By three o'clock that afternoon I was back at South-mere, helping Bettina with letters and phone calls in her small office off the foyer of the theater. Although her assistants at the box office were working effi-ciently, things were heating up before the opening performance of *La Traviata* the next evening, and she needed all the help she could get.

"Where's Simon?" I asked, noting that as usual he wasn't around when he might have been useful.

"He had some important deliveries to organize." With her big round eyes and curly dark hair, Bettina reminded me of Claudette Colbert in the reruns I'd seen of her early films.

I nodded neutrally, avoiding even a hint of criticism of precious Simon.

Bettina reported on the inquest that had been held that morning on the death of her uncle. They had presented James's deposition describing the finding of the body, the medical examiner had reported head injuries which were inconsistent with the fall from the tower, and the inquest had been speedily adjourned, as was the custom when the police needed more time to investigate.

Presently, Russell Ames strolled in, eyes blinking through his dark-rimmed glasses. Bettina was on the phone, and Russell exchanged with me an "Isn't she adorable?" look. We both smiled, and I gave him a cup of tea from the tray which had been brought in a few minutes earlier.

When Bettina finished her call, Russell grinned. "I've just had an encounter with Anton and I've come for tea and sympathy."

Bettina gave him one of her bone-melting looks. "Poor Russell! What is it this time?"

Russell took a swallow of tea. "In the third act, Anton wants Violetta to be in the act of changing her clothes during *'Addio del passato!'* "

I exploded. "She's already in a nightgown. What's she supposed to change to?"

"That's his point. He's been reading that consumptives sweat a good deal in the final stages, and he thinks it would be smashing for her to change to a fresh gown. Of course she would be wearing a little satin undergarment, he assured me, when she takes the gown over her head."

Bettina giggled. "What did you tell him, Russell?"

"I told him Ilena is only twenty-six and singing her first Violetta, and she's going to need her full concentration to sing the last big aria in the opera. Raising her arms and struggling in and out of nightgowns would tax a veteran singer, and he could forget it."

I asked, "Was he furious?"

"No, for once he didn't argue. Just looked disgusted and marched away."

As Russell waved farewell and strolled off, the phone, which had been silent for all of three minutes, rang now and I heard Bettina say, "Yes, Margot, of course. Yes, dear, I'll tell him the moment I see him."

When she rang off, I looked up in surprise. "Is Margot still here at Southmere? I'd have thought she'd be off to London by now."

"I thought so too—she seems so restless and at loose ends. But when I suggested she go up to town, she fairly snapped at me and said she prefers to stay here for the moment. Of course, it's easier for her to avoid the reporters here. In London they would dog her every footstep. Poor darling, I know she acts a bit flippant, Jane, but I'm sure she feels Julian's death most keenly."

"Of course," I murmured, toying with the figurines of the three monkeys which stood on Bettina's desk, exhorting the viewer to neither see, hear, nor speak evil. No use trying on cynicism with Bettina, the original "see no evil," so I merely said, "What did Margot want?"

"Oh, she wants Simon to do some sort of errand for her. She depends on him now that Julian's gone, you see."

I couldn't see Simon in the role of anybody's Rock of Gibraltar, but up until now, I had felt only mild irritation at his fecklessness. Later that evening, I had a view of Simon's character which did nothing to improve his image.

After dinner, I curled up in my robe and slippers in my room at the Dolphin and waited for James's nightly phone call. What he told me was not reassuring.

"About midday, the police asked me to come in to make a statement. Two of them cautioned me—again—and tried putting me on the griddle. I fended them off pretty well, darling, but it wasn't much fun being on the other side of the fence. I feel for my clients, I can tell you. You see, the police have nothing on which to hold me except their speculation, so of course they had to let me go.''

I fumed. "Margot could set them straight at once, couldn't she?"

"Precisely what I thought. I rang her up this afternoon and asked her to assure them there was nothing between us.''

"Yes?"

James sounded puzzled. "It's odd, but she asked if I had really lost all feeling for her, after—well, er—''

"Yes, dear, I understand. What did you say?"

"I said of course I am concerned for her as an old friend, but surely she understood that you and I care for each other very much and that I have no more—er—romantic feeling for her."

"And did she accept that?"

"Yes, I suppose she did. At least, she promised to tell the police what I said if they should ask her again.''

Oh, wonderful. I quelled an impulse to march straight off to Southmere and strangle Margot with my bare hands. To feed her ego, she was willing to let James be badgered by the police. But now James added something that took my mind off Margot.

"Do you remember, when Margot summoned me to her flat in London on the first occasion, she mentioned being concerned about some of Julian's associates? And I recommended the firm of investigators we sometimes use?''

"Yes."

"I asked her if she had in fact called upon them for help and she said she hadn't got round to it. Then when Julian died, of course it was no longer relevant. It seemed to me, Jane, that we might pursue that line ourselves, so I rang up Bolling Investigations and talked with a chap named MacDougal, whom I've worked with before. He came round for a chat, and tomorrow he'll be running down to Southmere to look over the scene and to talk with you. He'll look you up at the Dolphin in the afternoon. He's something of a character, but I believe you'll like him."

"I'll like anyone who can help us, darling. By the way, did you ever find out about the red-haired man, Mick Corcoran, who had the appointment at the tower with Julian the night he was killed?"

"Yes. I asked Detective Chief Inspector Collier why they weren't going after that chap instead of harassing me, and he said no harm in telling me. It seems Mr. Corcoran was eating shepherd's pie and playing darts in a pub in Burling from seven o'clock until about a quarter of nine that evening. The landlord and several patrons know him well, as he often takes a room upstairs there when he stays over in Burling."

"Oh, dear. Too bad!" Then I told James about my spur-of-the-moment visit that morning to Veeda Riley, editing slightly her remarks about Margot but giving him the full picture nevertheless. "Unfortunately, I didn't have the chance to ask her whether Julian might have been involved with any seedy characters, but I'll tell your Mr. MacDougal about her and see what he can find out. At least we're doing something!"

James said slowly, "What Mrs. Riley told you about Margot—about her being bitchy and so on."

"Yes?"

"It's true—she is like that. The odd thing is, I'd almost forgotten."

My sweet-natured James! Bitchiness would leave him hurt and baffled rather than angry. To change the subject, I asked, "Anything new on the Hawks case?"

"Hawks?" I could feel him swim back from painful memories of Margot. "Oh, Hawks. No. I've told him to keep his nose clean, and he seems to understand.

I'm afraid there's no doubt he and his chum were casing the neighborhood with intent to commit burglary when they were picked up. He'll have to live with his mother and behave himself for a time. He might even have to take a job!''

Just as I hung up the phone, I heard a tap at my door and found Simon Barnes standing in the passage. "Hello, Jane, may I come in?"

Alarmed, I said, "Of course! Is something wrong, Simon? Bettina—?"

"No, no." He closed the door behind him. "Everything's fine. I just dropped by to say hello."

"At this hour?"

I pulled my robe more firmly over my nightgown.

Simon stepped toward me, giving me what experience had no doubt taught him was an irresistible smile. He reminded me of one of those good-looking young Englishmen in a television commercial who model the latest thing in men's sweaters. He took me in a firm grip and bent down to start what was intended to be a lingering kiss.

When I recovered from the shock, I gave him a push. "Really, Simon, this is ridiculous!"

He seemed to take this as a gambit in a familiar game. "Come along, Jane." He pursed his lips and caressed my cheek with one finger. "You and James have been lovebirds for ages now. Isn't it time for a bit of harmless fun?"

"Extracurricular sex?" I said, with what I insisted as heavy irony.

His eyes lit with approval. "Exactly! Now you've got it!"

I retreated to one of a pair of chairs by a low table and Simon settled himself comfortably into the other.

"Look, Simon, you know I adore Bettina—"

"My dear Jane, I adore Bettina too. This has nothing to do with her."

"I hardly see the logic of that."

"You're not going to tell her, are you?"

He had me there. I wouldn't hurt Bettina for the world.

"Simon, let me talk to you as an old friend. When you married Bettina, I knew about Julian and the will, and I was glad that you seemed not to care about the money—"

He gave me a mocking grin. "Of course Julian gave her a tidy sum to be going on with. Besides, I was sure that eventually he'd weaken. One scarcely expected him to pop off so soon."

Exactly what James had said, only with less feeling. "Then you did marry Bettina, hoping for her legacy?"

"Oh, Jane, the little moralist. No, love, people marry for more complicated reasons than are dreamt of in your Puritan philosophy. Take James. Why did you marry him?"

I tried for flippancy. "I found his blue eyes irresistible."

"Of course you did. But James is a solicitor, and a rising one at that. What if those blue eyes had been the property of a punk rocker?"

"Really, Simon, you're impossible. Why are we having this conversation?"

He reached for my hand. "Jane, love, you look so sexy when you're annoyed."

I pulled my hand away and stood up. "Look, Simon, just bugger off."

His eyes crinkled in amusement. "You may not know it, but that's an extremely vulgar term."

"I've lived in this country long enough to know exactly how vulgar it is. That's why I used it."

"All right, Jane. You win. Sit down, sit down. I

promise to revert to kindly old Simon, beloved of dogs and children. So, tell me about James. Practice thriving and all that?"

"Yes."

"Doing any criminal practice, is he?"

"I wouldn't know. James never discusses his cases with me." This was my stock response to such questions. The truth was that James often told me about his cases, knowing that I would never discuss them with anyone.

Again the mocking smile. "What a proper little wench you are. Too good for the criminal client, is he?"

"No, I didn't say that."

"So he does take the odd criminal case, then? Ever had a murder?"

"No, I don't believe he has." Now I yawned and walked to the door, my hand on the knob. "Bye-bye time, Simon," I said firmly, and he went.

Later on, before drifting off to sleep I wondered if there had in fact been a purpose for Simon's visit—he wanted information. A picture flashed into my mind of Simon and me in bed together and my telling him, in postcoital confidence, about the Dan Hawks case, since this was the only criminal case James was handling at that time. Was I imagining things, or was this in fact the picture in Simon's mind when he made his rather silly attempt at seduction?

But why on earth should Simon want to know about James's case?

10

The next morning I awoke to what looked like a clear day, but by the time I went down to breakfast at the Dolphin, a dismal downpour had begun. As I lingered over my coffee, I was called to the telephone and heard Bettina's voice, sounding as near to exasperation as she ever got.

"Jane, dear, Riccardo just rang up. His car broke down somewhere out on the marshes and he's terrified he'll catch a chill and won't be able to sing tonight. Can you possibly—?"

"Of course. Just tell me where he is."

"Somewhere on the road to Burling Harbor, he said. Behind an old abandoned church." I consulted the hotel desk for directions, bundled into my rain gear, and set off to the car park. James had insisted that I take the car for the week, and it was indeed marvelous not to have to rely on taxis to buzz back and forth to Southmere as I had been doing previously.

Finding Riccardo proved to be easier than I had expected. I drove down to the main road, turned left and almost immediately left again at the signpost to Burling Harbor. There was actually only one road leading to the tiny harbor, where the rivers converged below the cliff and moved in a single sluggish flow toward the sea. Out on the flat land of the marsh, with the rain falling relentlessly from a forbidding sky of shifting blacks and grays, I shivered slightly, remembering that this desolate land had only a few centuries ago been under the sea. Even now, barren marsh grasses provided the chief vegetation, an occasional tree making a dark spot on the landscape.

As the road made a final turn and headed straight on toward the harbor, I saw on my right a steeple and soon the body of the ancient stone church came into view, and behind it a dilapidated house. Must once have been the vicarage, I thought. A narrow, muddy track led past the church and into a clearing in front of the house, where a rather battered van stood at one side. As I drew up near the entrance, Riccardo flung himself out of the door and scrambled into the passenger seat of the car, where I had the heater going full blast.

"Ah, Jane, you are the angel! Warm at last! The man at the house leaves me at the phone and goes off upstairs. There is no heat on the ground floor. You see, I shiver. I am whispering to save the voice."

I grinned, knowing all about singers' understandable obsessions. With pianists, I thought, it's the hands. A cut on the finger can be a disaster.

Riccardo's sibilant voice went on. "Darling Jane, what would become of me without you?"

"Someone else would have come, Riccardo. But what were you doing out here?"

"I wake up early and the weather looked good, so I go for a drive. I wonder what the marsh is like and how far to the sea by road, yes?"

"Yes."

"Then the rain pour down and the car go sput-sput

and the motor die out. Then it refuse to start up again. I see the house but I think no one live there. Then I see the van and I run to the door. The man does not like to let me in, but I explain and he let me use the telephone."

"I see." As the road made a turn and the old house and church appeared on our left, we both looked in that direction. What happened then was so startling that it seemed as unreal as something in a dream. We saw a flash of light, and the house burst into a ball of flame and billowing smoke. Then, a measurable second later, we heard the muted booming sound of the explosion. Without a second thought, I braked and began to turn the car when I heard Riccardo cry out, "No, Jane, no! Don't go back!"

I stared. "Of course we must go back. Someone may need help!" I sped back along the road and into the drive leading to the burning house.

It was not a pretty sight. Pieces of roofing, chunks of walls, fragments of what may have been chairs and tables, lay scattered about on the barren ground, where no garden had been cultivated. While the upper story of the house was nearly decimated, part of the ground floor, including the entry door, was still intact. When I ran to the door I found it locked, but I noticed the glass in a low window to the left of the door had shattered, and I picked my way across to the sash, knocking away a few shards of glass with my gloved hands so that I could see inside.

"Is anyone there?" I shouted. Now I could feel the heat from the flames that engulfed the upper story of the house. At the same time, the rain poured down my neck, and I could hear its wild hissing as it met the fire above. When I shouted again, I saw a section of the stairway buckle, and I turned and ran for the car, which I had left at a safe distance, as another roar announced the collapse of the interior of the house.

I stood staring helplessly as the fire spread, when a car appeared in the drive and a man leaped out. "Anything I can do?"

I shook my head. "It looks pretty hopeless. There was a man in there a few minutes ago but I don't see anyone now."

"Do you know who lives here?"

"No, we were just passing. Shall we go for help?"

The man looked toward the town of Burling, perched on the cliff above the marshland. "No, I've already rung up for the fire brigade in Burling. They don't have a permanent staff, but their chaps have beepers and they'll be here in jig time. The rain may have the flames out before they arrive."

I would have thought so too, but I noticed that the fire burned stubbornly on despite the downpour.

Now two men in another car joined us in the drive, where we all stood staring at the shattered and burning remains of the house. The late arrivals, who were locals, explained that the old house had been abandoned for years. Noticing the rather battered van parked there recently, they had suspected squatters but did nothing.

"None of our affair, is it?" said an elderly man with the weather-beaten face of a fisherman. "Let the police deal with it, I say."

"Rrrrr," said his companion in what I took to be assent.

I wondered if squatters would have a telephone, but like the fisherman, I decided it wasn't my problem.

Learning that a man had been in the upper story shortly before the fire, they shook their heads.

"Not much left of the poor chap now, I'd say."

"Must have been tinkering with one of them oil heaters, and it blew up on him or summat."

Now we heard the sound of the approaching fire engine and stepped quickly to our cars to move them out of the way. I nearly jumped when I saw Riccardo cowering in the passenger seat. In the excitement I had forgotten him. Fortunately for his health, I had left the motor running and hence the heater had kept him thoroughly warm.

"Ah, Jane, such courage! I am the coward, you see. I do not wish to be hurt."

I looked at him and grinned. "Neither do I, Riccardo. You noticed I ran like a rabbit when I could see the house was about to collapse!"

"Do we leave now?"

I saw the fire crew had arrived and were going about their task. "Yes, why not? No use hanging about gawking."

After dropping Riccardo at a garage to arrange to have his car rescued, I went on to Bettina's little office at the theater. I found her looking rather distraught.

"All's well with Caruso," I assured her. "Is the pressure getting to you, poor lamb?"

"No, it's not that, Jane. It's the police. They've been at the house this morning, questioning Simon again."

At the mention of Simon, I felt a warm flush begin to creep up my face, remembering his visit to my room the night before. Damn him, anyway, I thought. Why should *I* feel uncomfortable when I was in no way to blame? I bent down and twiddled with my shoe to hide my awkwardness.

This was the first I had heard of Simon being under suspicion. Raising my head, I asked Bettina, "What do they want with Simon?"

"You see, Simon can't prove exactly where he was at the time Uncle Julian was—that is, at the time he died."

"Yes, come to think of it, where was he?" Since Simon would have every reason for wanting Julian to survive and leave Bettina some money, I hadn't seriously considered him as a prime suspect.

"He was in our bedroom at the house until after seven o'clock. He had been out making a delivery and had to bathe and change. Just as he came along toward the theater, he saw the ambulance taking Uncle Julian away. Of course, he didn't know it was Uncle until he came round to the stage door and learned what had happened. Then he took Margot to the hospital, as you know."

"Yes, I see. Most of us were here in the theater in pretty plain view of each other at the time. I suppose the police are eager to latch on to anyone who was unaccounted for, like Simon—or James." I had made light to Bettina of their suspicion of James, to spare her worry.

Without telling her that I had seen Simon in a lorry with a man resembling Corcoran, I asked innocently, "What about the fellow Mick Corcoran, who said he had an appointment with Julian? Does anyone know who he is?"

"Yes, he is an associate of Simon in the company."

"Then, if Simon knows Corcoran, he must know what his appointment with Julian was about?"

Bettina looked down at her desk, shuffling papers with hands that trembled slightly. "Simon says it was something about the business."

"What does Corcoran say?"

"He says Julian wanted some freight transported for the theater."

"Why on earth would they meet at night by the tower?"

Bettina sighed. "I don't know, Jane."

"Well, look, Bettina, Simon hadn't a reason in the world for wanting Julian out of the way, so don't worry. It will all blow over soon."

Her huge eyes still troubled, Bettina sighed again as the phone rang and we plunged back into the work of the day:

At lunch time, I went back to the Dolphin and had a sandwich sent up to my room, where I switched on the television to the midday news. In the portion giving news of the southeast, there was a picture of the smoking ruins of the house on the marsh and the grisly announcement that the remains of a body had been found in the wreckage but no description was possible. Police were investigating the cause of the explosion. A telephone for that address was listed to an Oliver Brown. Persons having information about the house or its occupants were requested to notify the authorities.

I rang up Riccardo's room at the Dolphin to report what I had just heard. "You could describe the man who let you use the telephone, Riccardo. Shall I ring them up?"

A strangled shriek greeted this suggestion. "The police? No, Jane, no! I have nothing to say to police. You tell them nothing!"

"All right, I'm sure someone else will come forward and let you off the hook. How are you feeling?"

"I think the voice is good. I have been warming up and it seems to be there."

"Good, good. Take care, Riccardo."

A few minutes later, I went down to the lounge to meet the investigator whom James had hired and who had rung me up that morning for an appointment at two o'clock. For some reason, I had expected a sort of sporting type, with a checked coat and loud tie. The man who rose to meet me wore a nondescript tweed suit, plain tie, and brown loafers somewhat the worse for wear. His face was etched with lines, from the forehead with its horizontal bands and two deep frown marks between the brows to the grooves which ran from cheekbones to chin. He might have been any age from forty to sixty.

"Mrs. Hall? I'm Ian MacDougal."

I smiled. "I've ordered coffee. Would you like something else?"

"Coffee's fine, thank you."

When he sat down, he bent forward till his arms rested on his knees and looked up at me out of smallish, neutral-colored eyes. "Time we put our heads together, eh? Can't have the coppers bothering Mr. H., now can we?"

"You do believe he's innocent, then?"

He eyed me shrewdly. "Don't you?"

"I *know* he is, Mr. MacDougal."

"Just MacDougal, Mrs. H." He nodded. He took out a small notebook and pen. "Now then."

"What can I tell you?"

"To start off, I'd like to know about your chat with the lady named Veeda Riley. I've had the picture from Mr. H. about her relation to Mr. Kingsley and so on. What was your impression of her?"

I recounted in some detail my conversation with Veeda, including her cryptic remark at the end that "they" wouldn't let her keep the money she would receive from Julian's will. James had said on the phone that there was no legal impediment to her receiving the money. Now I asked MacDougal if he had any clue to what she might have meant.

82

"Sounds as if she has family members who may try to take it away from her."

"Yes. She said 'my—' and then broke off. The problem is, she impressed me as a lady who could look after her own interests and wouldn't be easily pushed around."

"Mmm. I'll nose about."

Now MacDougal asked for an account of the people who were present at the time of Julian's murder. Bent nearly double over his knees, he took careful notes, asking for spelling of names and elucidation of details as I described everyone who was on the premises of the theater that evening.

"Now for the scene of the crime, Mrs. H."

We finished our coffee and set off for Southmere where I gave him a tour of the tower, leading the way up the twisting stone steps with the aid of the torch which was kept inside the entrance door. On the terrace, MacDougal stood with his back to the balustrade and looked at me challengingly. "Try to push me off, Mrs. H."

After a startled glance, I understood and stepped toward him to try to grasp his shoulders. His arms shot out and pinioned my wrists while he raised one foot in readiness to kick his attacker.

"Not so easy, eh? Even if you were a good deal larger and stronger than I am, you'd have a job to heave me over. I understand our Mr. Kingsley was tall and fit, not one of your weaklings."

"Yes."

"Our chap must surely have zapped him first, as the police seem to think. Now for a gander at the theater, Mrs. H."

On our way down the hill, MacDougal entertained me with an account of the advantages of his appearance.

"In my line of work, it's no good looking dashing. Someone says, 'Can you describe the man you saw, madam?' 'Oh, yes,' she says, 'he was sort of medium height, not fat or thin, medium brown hair.' 'Eyes?' 'I can't really say. Sort of hazel, I think.' "

"And how about speech?" I said. "You don't sound a bit Scottish, MacDougal."

"Right. I was Edinburgh born and bred, but I worked out all the accent till I sound as flat as a Yank, begging your pardon, Mrs. H."

I laughed. "I'm a hybrid, I'm afraid. I sound American to everyone here, but when I visit my home in California, they tease me for sounding Brit."

When we reached the theater, I led the way through the stage door entrance to the spot where I had stood some time before seven o'clock on the night of Julian's death. The members of the stage crew who were already at work on the sets for tonight's performance utterly ignored us and went about their tasks with the lackadaisical air which always left me astonished that the sets actually appeared intact and on time.

MacDougal found a folding chair and took out his notebook. "It appears that our chap Kingsley was murdered some time between seven o'clock and a quarter past, when Mr. H. arrived from London and came upon the body by the tower. So where was everyone at that time?"

I pointed to the box above stage left. "When I came into the wings here, Margot—Mrs. Kingsley—was there in the box with her husband. I was absorbed in watching the rehearsal when I heard her tell him angrily to go. Russell Ames, the conductor, was in the pit with the orchestra. It was nearing the end of the first act. The soprano, Ilena Santos, was on stage alone, doing her big aria. The designer-director, Anton Szabo, was in the house, just under the Kingsleys' box. He had stopped the rehearsal moments before to give some directions to the chorus. Bettina Barnes, Mr. Kingsley's niece, was standing here near me.

"As for the others, the baritone, Riccardo Palma, must have been in his dressing room, as Germont doesn't come in until the second act. The tenor, Dmitri Mikos, would be waiting to come back in for the final duet. Ilena's husband, Dr. Raymond Flynt, was in the stalls after the ambulance had gone, but I can't say where he was before that. Bettina's husband, Simon Barnes, claims that he was in the main house at Southmere and came across just as the ambulance was leaving."

As MacDougal finished his last note, his hands dropped between his knees and he sat in brooding silence, head bent. Then he sprang briskly to his feet. "Righto, Mrs. H. Plenty of work to do. As our friend Milton says, we must scorn delights and live laborious days!"

11

That evening I set off early for the theater, taking Riccardo along, as his car was still in the garage.

"I tell you, Jane," He began with a sputter, "Miss Ilena better hold her position tonight or I'll wring her pretty small neck. At dress rehearsal, you *saw* how she try to upstage me, did you not?"

"Mmm," I murmured. He was quite right but I wanted none of their squabbles.

Taking this for agreement, he plunged on. "First scene of second act is *mine*, is it not? She is star of the whole show, but Germont has this one great scene. Yet during my *'Pura siccome un angelo,'* Ilena is throwing herself about on the stage. I ask Szabo to speak to her but he say it's not natural for her to be still. Thank God, Russell Ames understands. He says she should show emotion in her face but sit quiet. Than Szabo agrees and tells Ilena to keep still. Also, in the duet, she must keep her positions, yes?"

"Mmm."

Now he lowered his voice to his confidential gossipy tone. "And how she carries on. You see her everywhere with Dmitri, and her husband, the doctor, he sees nothing and smiles all the time. It was the same in Salzburg, Jane, only it was not Dmitri.''

I remembered that it was in Salzburg that Julian had scouted both Ilena and Riccardo, where they were singing supporting roles in Mozart's *Cosi fan tutte*.

Riccardo placed a friendly hand on my knee as I drove. "I tell you this in strictest confidence, Jane. I never tell anyone before. It was Mr. Kingsley she was carrying on with in Salzburg!''

"Julian?" I was surprised, not because I put it past Julian to have a fling, but because I hadn't heard this nugget before.

Riccardo nodded solemnly, removing his hand from my knee to readjust the woolen scarf around his neck. "Yes. And the Dr. Raymond, he was there also and never noticed a thing but looked happy as the lark. Then Mrs. Kingsley arrived and all is proper while she is there.''

I gave a noncommital "hmm," but Riccardo needed no encouragement to burble on. "Then Anton Szabo come and Mrs. Kingsley is very friendly to him. I am surprised when I come here and see how they dislike each other and I wonder what happened because in Salzburg six months ago, they are on good terms. I see them one day in a little café across the river, having the drink and laughing in most friendly fashion.''

I wondered if Anton was the only man in creation who hadn't fallen at Margot's feet, a transgression she would never forgive.

Backstage at the theater, Riccardo persisted in telling everyone about our morning's adventure with the burning house on the marsh, making me out to be a female version of Horatio at the bridge.

"Stop it, Riccardo," I protested. "You make me sound such a fool." I had never felt inclined to risk my life to rescue a stranger, and I had asked myself since the morning whether my instinctive return to the burning house was more foolhardy than sensible. At any rate, I had retreated when I saw there was no one lying helpless on the premises.

The performance of *La Traviata* went off without a glitch, the principals all singing like angels. Ilena and Dmitri derived real pathos from their love scenes, making the most of the familiar lines:

> *Amor è palpito*
> *Dell'universo—*

"Love is the breath of the universe," as one rather free translation has it. Some might say this was old-hat nineteenth-century sentimentality, but I had noticed that, hard-boiled as our society liked to think of itself, most people found that love still carried a pretty good clout.

While Riccardo soared in his second act aria, I looked again with astonishment at Anton Szabo's sets for what was presumed to be the lovers' idyllic hideaway in the country. Right of center stood a wooden structure, square at the bottom and narrowing upward, looking for all the world like a small oil derrick. A series of five-foot-wide backdrop curtains, split and tattered along the edges, depicted parts of human bodies: eyes with giant lashes, female legs, hairy arms, faceless heads with swatches of hair. Downstage left a crude bench was placed in front of an empty door frame.

To her disgust, Ilena's costume was a cheap, red satin gown, companion to the black one she had worn in the first act, because Anton insisted that as a Paris prostitute "she wouldn't own any other clothes."

For the following scene, in which Alfredo plays cards with the Baron, Anton had designed a dingy café instead of the richly furnished Paris salon of Violetta's friend Flora. He had cut the dancing at the opening of the scene, substituting some horseplay among the "gypsies" and "matadors" which was singularly inappropriate to the words of the libretto, but that didn't bother Anton.

During the intermissions, I mingled with the audience and heard praise for the music but a good many grumbles about the staging. One man said "Damn silly, if you ask me" and was countered by his wife's timid voice, "I suppose they want to do something *different*, dear."

While it was clear that no one actually *liked* Anton Szabo's trendy interpretation, the fear of being regarded as an old fogey stalked the mental corridors of those who liked to think of themselves as in with the latest craze, whatever it might be. The same concern applied to the critics, some of whom would no doubt support anything that looked even remotely avantgarde. Besides, for those suffering from professional fatigue after having reviewed countless *Traviatas,* it gave them something new to write about.

After the performance, there was another gathering at Mario's, larger than the one after the opening of *Turn,* and our host had obligingly set additional tables. This time Simon turned up, oozing charm and being gratifyingly attentive to Bettina. In the vague shuffling for places, Riccardo and his ladylove from the chorus, to whom I had given a lift back to town, were sitting at my left, while Anton Szabo, who had evidently decided for once to socialize, dropped into the chair at my right.

Unable to rave to Anton about the sets or the staging, I simply echoed the general acclaim that the opening performance had been a smash. I needn't have worried about the omission. Anton's ego was such that he took all praise as a personal tribute.

His dark eyes, beneath the crown of black curls, sizzled at me. "Good thing to shake 'em up, I say. Some old farts from the press will gripe that we didn't have pretty costumes and all that shit, but who listens to them?"

As he turned to study the menu, I reflected on my good luck in keeping my own opinions hidden without having to bend the truth. When I wrote the program notes for the operas, I had sidestepped on *Traviata* by the simple device of presenting a lengthy interview with Anton, faithfully quoting his diatribes about "relevance" and "symbol," and the need for "opening new perspectives" on the "fusty" world of Verdi. It wasn't my job to evaluate.

What an odd creature Anton was, I thought. His slender body, vibrant with energy, suggested a man with a powerful sexual drive, yet I had never heard a mention of wife or girlfriend. In his early thirties and already launched on a promising career in theater as well as opera, Anton seemed to exist entirely in the cocoon of his work. Certainly, he had little interest in people. He forgot their names, walked off abruptly in the midst of conversations, and generally gave the impression that he would knife his own grandmother if it would help him to get ahead.

When we had placed our orders, I was about to turn to Riccardo and his friend, expecting no conversation from Anton, when he surprised me by fixing me with that piercing look. "Jane, you're from the States, right?"

"Yes."

"East or West Coast?"

"Los Angeles, Anton." I had mentioned this on

several occasions but of course he had forgotten. Now I learned why it suddenly registered.

"I had a phone call from my agent today. One of the big universities there wants me to do a series of lectures on stage and opera design and direction. What do you know about Southern California University?"

I grinned. "Only that I did my Ph.D. in music there!"

"You're kidding!" I had his full attention now, if only briefly. "So tell me about it. I didn't know much about the West Coast when I was in New Haven."

I nearly giggled. No one who went there ever said the name of Yale University, just as an Englishman never spoke of Oxford or Cambridge, but only the name of his college.

"What can I say? It's not Harvard or the Other Place, but its graduate schools are pretty well known."

"You must have some contacts there?"

"Well, I know the music faculty, of course, as well as a few from other departments. My own professor was Dr. Andrew Quentin. Actually, he's coming to England this week and plans to get down here to Southmere to see both operas on Friday and Saturday. I'll see that you meet."

While I didn't really see what Andrew could tell him, I knew Anton to be an ardent networker who liked to have contacts in his pocket wherever he went.

"Great, great!" he exclaimed, but lapsed almost at once into moody silence, his attention span having evidently reached its limit. When the food arrived, Anton, without another word, wolfed down his linguini and bolted off, tossing a sketchy "See ya" over his shoulder.

The next morning, I took up Bettina on her offer of a free half day and had a late breakfast in my room at the Dolphin. With both opening nights out of the way, the pressure was off at Southmere. Tonight's second performance of *The Turn of the Screw* should present no problems, and from here on the administrative work would settle into a routine in the final days of the festival.

When my phone rang, I heard the flat, noncommittal voice of the private investigator, Ian MacDougal.

"Good morning, Mrs. H. A question for you. What do you know about the City Freight Services, Ltd., and the connection between Mr. Simon Barnes and Mr. Mick Corcoran, as you and Mr. H. mentioned?"

"Not much at all, I'm afraid. Simon seems to come and go at odd hours, and we know nothing about the man Corcoran except that he seems to have an iron-clad alibi for the time of Julian's death."

"I see. I've been on the phone this morning and getting some odd answers. When I told the young lady in the London office I needed transport for a large consignment of motor equipment coming into London and all our regular chaps were booked up, she hemmed and hawed and said I must speak to Mr. Corcoran, only he was out and might not return today. What kind of business is that, I ask you? It has a strong whiff of the fishmonger, I'd say."

"Yes, doesn't it? Of course I've noticed that Simon has always been vague about his activities, but I rather assumed it was dereliction of duty on his part. He's not keen on hard work. And I don't believe his wife knows much more about it than I do."

"Righto. I'm off, then. Thank you, Mrs. H., and get in touch if you learn anything."

Looking out my window, I saw that yesterday's rain had gone, and the patchy clouds lured me out for a brisk walk after breakfast. Warmly bundled as I was from toe to head, only my nose informed me that the temperature was down in the low forties. My leather boots eased the pressure of the cobblestones as I climbed the hill past Lamb House and skirted the gravestones in the churchyard, circling the oval, brick water reservoir and the parish church, with its flying buttresses, then back along Watchman Street with its fine old houses, to the lookout point on the south cliff. There, beyond the marsh, lay the sea, a band of gray under the gloomy sky.

I could make out a handful of fishing boats in the little harbor of Burling, and now that I knew where to look, I could see the old stone church and behind it, the spot where yesterday's explosion had decimated the house and killed its occupant. As I turned and meandered down a narrow passage toward the lower part of the town, I wondered about the man, Oliver Brown, who had signed up for telephone service at the abandoned house. Was Brown the same man who had reluctantly allowed Riccardo to use the phone? Or was this another person occupying the house?

When I rounded the corner at the bottom of the hill, I glanced to my left into a cul-de-sac and was startled to see a small lorry, dark green and lettered in white with the words City Freight Services, Ltd., parked across the end of the alley, its tailgate lowered to form a ramp. Thinking for a moment this was an extraordinary coincidence, I realized it was nothing of the sort. Even though the headquarters of Simon's firm was in London, the lorry had every reason to be here while he was in residence at Southmere. If I hadn't just spoken with MacDougal, I'd have passed on without a second thought.

Instead, I walked down the lane, and seeing no one about, climbed swiftly up the ramp and into the body of the truck. A number of large crates stood toward the back, some against the side wall, others stacked near the high wooden barrier that separated this area from the cab. I tried to pry open the tops of those nearest me but found them securely fastened. Moving to the back, I was bending over to read the label stencilled on the side of the largest of the crates when I heard voices and footsteps.

What on earth could I say if Simon appeared? All I could think of was something inane, such as having seen a cat run into the lorry and trying to rescue it. Instinctively, I ducked behind the crate as I heard the sounds of a heavy object being carried up the ramp and deposited, with grunts of satisfaction, in the body of the lorry. It's simple, I thought. I'll wait till they go for the next load and then slip quietly away.

Simon's voice put an end to that plan. "That's it, Mick," he said, and a moment later, the ramp had been raised, and chains rattled as it was fastened in place. Now, darkness descended on the interior as a canvas was rolled down and evidently hooked to the top of the tailgate.

It was now or never. Whatever the awkwardness, I *must* call out to Simon, yet I found myself absolutely paralyzed. I squeezed into the narrow space between the crates, my back to the wall, as the motor started and the lorry moved away. Oh well, I thought, maybe they will say something that will give me some information, but someone switched on the radio to blaring rock music, and the two men drove on without exchanging a word.

12

At first I simply cowered into the confined space behind the crates as the lorry lumbered its way, with many twists and turns, out of the town of Burling. Then my head cleared and I began to think about where we were headed.

Soon, the smoother running of the wheels told me we were on a main road. But in which direction? Uphill, certainly, as the motor labored noisily and we began to swing around curves. That meant north on the London Road, since the road to the east and west of Burling ran along the flat marsh for some miles. Well, if I had to sit here all the way to London, so be it. Maybe they would stop for coffee somewhere. But even so, would I be able to climb out of my prison?

Looking up, I could see Simon's head, with its wavy dark hair, above me on the driver's side, while at his left, only the top of Mick Corcoran's carroty locks was visible. I longed to creep to the back of the lorry, where I could peer out in the gap between the canvas and the top of the tailgate, but if Simon turned his head, he could hardly fail to see me. Better stay put.

In a few minutes, I had hit upon my strategy if my

presence was detected. Dazed and confused, I would confess that I had suffered since childhood from occasional attacks of amnesia and had no idea how I came to be where I was. It was pretty thin but it was the best I could do.

Presently, I felt the lorry make a sharp turn and soon begin to lurch over an exceedingly bumpy road. The deafening music was switched off in mid-rock, and blissful silence descended, except for the grinding sounds of the motor. Wherever we were, I thanked whatever gods there be that this was certainly not the road to London.

The lorry slowed to a crawl, and at last I heard Simon speak. "It must be along here somewhere. 'Down in a hollow,' he said. He's always maundering on about the old days and the smuggling and what not, and this time I pricked up my ears, I can tell you. When we lost poor old Ollie's place, I thought we were up the spout.''

Corcoran muttered something I didn't catch and Simon cried, "That's it, all right.''

The truck ground to a stop and both men jumped from the cab where I could hear them walking forward. Gingerly, I stood up and peered over the divider and through the windscreen.

Now I could see that we were in thick woods, with only a small clearing in a hollow a few yards ahead. Simon and Corcoran were beating back heavy brush in front of what looked like a metal box, about two feet by three, standing next to a tree trunk. Once uncovered, the box was revealed to have a hinged top which the two men, with some difficulty, managed to pull open.

Simon's head turned and I ducked down, a pulse in my neck throbbing, my hands icy inside their gloves. At this point, a child of ten would have deduced that this was a cache for some kind of illegal trafficking, and my being found here was not merely embarrassing but downright dangerous.

Following my plan, I slipped down behind the crates and lay still, ready to close my eyes and feign sleep at the first chance of detection. To my surprise, all was silent. No voices, no footsteps, for what seemed an eternity. Then at last I heard the two men walking to the back of the lorry, followed by the welcome jangle of chains and the thud as the tailgate dropped into the soft, rain-soaked earth.

Working in what was no doubt an accustomed rhythm, the men lifted a crate which must have been heavy, as I could hear little gusts of breath as they went down the ramp and along the side of the lorry, not more than a foot from where I lay. The impulse to escape was so great that I had to force myself to wait until I was sure they had reached the cache. Then, without risking another glimpse through the wind-screen, I crept toward the back of the lorry, treading as softly as I could down the ramp.

Now for the bad moment. On either side of the lorry I saw inviting thickets in the woods, but if either of the men should look back, I could be seen as I made my break for freedom. I stood irresolute for a terrifying moment, then put my head around the side for a quick look. Nothing! No one in sight.

My heart began to hammer and I nearly cried out. How could two men and a heavy crate simply disappear? Involuntarily, I remembered the ghosts in *The Turn of the Screw*, appearing and vanishing as the young governess watched in horror. With a shudder, I turned and ran up the hill and into the woods on the far side of the lorry, crashing through the underbrush in mindless terror. Then I heard a sound, and crouching behind a thick screen of fern, I looked down the hill in time to see Simon's head emerging from the metal box by the tree. Stepping out, he turned and offered a hand to his companion who was obviously climbing a ladder leading from some sort of underground vault.

So much for my ghosts. Such hiding places must have been fairly common in the heyday of smuggling in the seventeenth and eighteenth centuries, not only in Burling but all over the south coast of England. Feeling like a proper fool, I settled down in my nest, safely screened from view, and watched while Simon and Corcoran deposited two more crates in their hiding place, then closed the top, piled shrubbery over the opening, and retreated to their lorry, backing up the lane until they found a place to turn. Then, at last, the grinding of the motor died away.

Five minutes later I emerged from the narrow lane and found myself on the London Road, near the crest of a hill. The roofs and chimneys of Southmere were visible on my right, confirming what I had begun to suspect: that Simon's underground cache was somewhere on the grounds of the Kingsley place. With a shrug, I turned to my left and trudged the mile or so back to Burling and the Dolphin, where I blissfully sank into a hot bath.

While I was dressing, I rang up MacDougal's office to report the results of my sleuthing. The receptionist told me he was out but she would reach him on his beeper and have him ring me back. In no time, he was on the line, chortling over my account of the morning's adventure.

"Mrs. H., you are the one! We can use you in the business if you'd like a change of occupation."

I laughed. "Thanks, Mr. MacDougal, but I think I'll stick to music."

"Righto. I'd like to have a look at your smugglers' hideaway. If I come down to Burling tomorrow morning about a quarter past eight, will that suit? I'll leave London at six to avoid the worst of the traffic."

"Yes, fine. If you'll come here to the Dolphin, I'll take you out to the place. I'm sure I can find it."

"Now, now, Mrs. H., you'll do no such thing. You can describe it to me but you're not going near there. You had a lucky escape today but we'll not risk that again. It's too dangerous. If your chaps happen to come upon *me,* there's no connection with you, do you see? I'll feed them a line, all right."

I saw his point and offered no further objection.

Before going to Southmere for the afternoon, I went along to the High Street for a light lunch in a tea shop, where I had no sooner ordered than Raymond and Ilena wandered in and joined me.

I smiled. "No performance till Friday, Ilena."

Her pretty face wore its usual sulky look. "Yes, it is nice to have two days' rest."

"You were really marvelous last night!"

Now a smile broke through the gloom. "Thank you, dear Jane."

Raymond beamed as always. "Her first Violetta. A big milestone, right?"

"Right."

Ilena studied the brief menu, looking up at Raymond uncertainly. "Would I like a watercress sandwich?"

Raymond glanced at the card and spoke decisively. "No, no. Have the cheese and ham. Better for you, more filling."

I realized that I had never seen these two together without other people around, either in a group or with Dmitri hanging about. Now I was struck with Raymond's casual manner with her and her obvious air of dependence. Perhaps it was the difference in their ages. Raymond looked to be pushing forty, at least a dozen years older than his wife, I surmised.

Looking out at the overcast sky, Ilena shivered. "Don't you miss Los Angeles, Jane? It will feel so good to be back in the sunshine."

"When I first came to live in England, I did miss the warm weather, but not now. I knew I had become a native when I found myself sitting around in the flat wearing two sweaters instead of turning up the heat!"

Raymond stroked his beard. "Man's capacity for adaptation is extraordinary. Think of the Indian mystics who not only walk on coals but reduce their need for food to an incredible minimum."

I laughed. "I'd never make it to that extreme, Raymond. My tastes are too sybaritic."

We chatted idly through lunch, and I was about to take my leave when Raymond put a hand on my arm. "No, wait, Jane. There's something I want to talk to you about."

Surprised, I said "All right," and poured myself a final cup of tea.

Then Raymond turned to Ilena. "You go ahead. I'll be along soon. Dmitri will be waiting for you."

Ilena's dark eyes looked into Raymond's face, which for once was not displaying his fixed grin. Then she told me goodbye and went slowly out of the tea shop where she stood for a moment on the pavement, her head lowered, before starting up the hill toward the Dolphin.

"What is it, Raymond?" I asked.

I felt as if Ilena had been dismissed so the grownups could talk, and since I was only a couple of years older than his wife, I wasn't sure I was flattered by Raymond's assumption of my advanced age.

Now Raymond's teeth were bared in the eternal

smile. "She and Dmitri play gin rummy by the hour. She'll be okay."

Pouring milk into my tea, I repressed the impulse to remark on his complacency.

Raymond asked for another Perrier, with ice. "Now, Jane, here's the problem. I don't want to worry Ilena, but the police have been badgering me about where I was when Julian was—that is, when he died."

I had been through this same conversation with Riccardo—why did everyone have to confide in me?— so I asked Raymond the obvious question. "Come to think of it, where were you?"

"I was in a box in the second tier, watching the rehearsal. I was hoping you might have noticed me there and could get the hounds off my back."

"I'm sorry, Raymond, but I'm afraid I didn't see you."

"I can't think of anyone else who might help me. The house was darkened, so no one on the stage could see that far back. Szabo was all over the place, but I asked him and he's hopeless. He said his mind was on the performance and he wouldn't have noticed if the whole royal family had turned up in a box. God, I was counting on you, Jane. Think, now. I saw you down in the stalls. Then you left and went through to the wings. You might have glanced back and seen me then?"

I shook my head. "Afraid not. After James came, we both saw you in the stalls, but that's no help. Julian was already dead by that time. Were you in the center or on the side?"

"Sort of in the center but where it curves."

"On the opposite side from Margot and Julian?"

"No, on the same side."

"Hmm. Then did you hear Julian when he left the box? He would have walked along the passage past your box, wouldn't he?"

"Yes, the police asked me that too, but I didn't hear a thing. The carpet is a foot thick along there, you know. Julian didn't spare the horses when he fixed up the theater."

"But Raymond, what motive could you have for murdering Julian?"

"None at all. That's what I keep telling them. He gave Ilena a great role. Why would I want to do the poor bastard in?"

Of course I remembered Riccardo's gossip about Ilena and Julian in Salzburg, but I could hardly believe that a flirtation six or eight months ago would constitute a motive for Raymond at this late date. There certainly had been no hint of anything between Ilena and Julian here at Southmere.

I tried to reassure Raymond that without a motive he should be in the clear. As I drove on to the theater I reflected that James seemed to be the only suspect with both opportunity and what the police, at any rate, regarded as a motive.

When at last I reached Bettina's office off the foyer of the Southmere Theater, I was surprised to see Margot Kingsley there, sitting in the chair I usually occupied.

I hadn't seen Margot since the reading of Julian's will three days earlier when she had scarcely looked like the bereaved and pining widow. Now her whole body sagged and her voice was listless as she said "Hello." Except for twisting a ring round and round her finger, she made no other movement.

I took one look at her drawn, almost haggard, face and felt a tiny stab of pity. Had I been wrong? Had the shock of Julian's death reached her in a delayed reaction?

Now Bettina arrived, breathless and smiling.

"Hello, darlings. Sorry I'm late. Simon and I lunched at the Tandoori place—delicious! You really should have come, Margot. I think the vultures have given up for the moment."

We had all worked hard in the days since Julian's death to shield Margot from the press. I nodded in agreement. "Unless some diehard is hiding in the shrubbery, I think we've driven them off."

Bettina's mention of Simon renewed the mental debate that had plagued me since my morning's discovery. Did I owe it to Bettina to tell her about her husband's obviously illegal activities, hoping to put a stop to it before he found himself in prison? Or should I remember the dismal fate, in Greek drama, of the bearer of evil tidings, and say nothing? I must talk it over with James.

Back at her desk, Bettina took up a large checkbook and a sheaf of papers. "It's so good of you to come here, Margot dear. I could have brought all this to the house."

Again, the lifeless tone. "It doesn't matter. It's as well to get out for a bit. I would have come to lunch but I'm not hungry."

Bettina gave me a "poor Margot" look, her enormous eyes filled with pity. "Here we are then. I've written a series of checks for your signature, now that the bank has cleared the account. Here is the list of what each one is for—"

For a moment, Margot sat staring at the sapphire and diamond ring on her right hand. Then she took up the pen. "I needn't look at all that. Just give me the checks."

As Margot signed, I had a vivid awareness of the really enormous sums of money over which this young woman would soon have control. Naively, I had thought that the police, cynical as they must be in their line of work, would at least question whether a man like James would commit murder in order to renew his relationship with his old flame, no matter how alluring she was. Why not simply have an affair with her? Belatedly, I saw the whole thing from the outsider's point of view—not love, but money. With Julian out of the way, James could divorce me and be in line for untold millions of pounds.

When Margot had finished signing and rose to go, I excused myself to Bettina and followed Margot out to the foyer. Why not? I thought. What can I lose?

"Margot, I'd like to speak to you, please."

She stopped and said, "Yes?" without bothering to turn.

"Will you please tell the police quite clearly that James was *not* trying to renew an intimate relationship with you when he came to see you in your flat in Mayfair?"

Now she turned to face me, the listless expression gone, her eyes icy with anger. "But, darling, I *have* told them. I can't help it if the oafs choose not to believe me."

And she swept off.

Back in the little office, it was all I could do not to pour out the whole story to Bettina, who innocently pursued the tale of Margot's suffering. "Old Alfred tells me that Margot has taken to walking out at night. When he locks up, he leaves the pantry door locked but not chained, and she lets herself in with her key. Of course, Simon and I hear nothing, as we're in the other wing."

The ringing of the phone saved me from having to comment, and we spent the afternoon coping with the routine problems of the festival.

That evening, after the second successful performance of *The Turn of the Screw*, I hurried back to the

Dolphin to talk with James on the phone, telling him the story of my incarceration in the lorry and what I had learned about Simon and Mick Corcoran.

"What on earth shall we do about Simon?" I asked. "We'll have to come up with some solution, for Bettina's sake."

James pondered. "Look, darling, one thing is clear. If you must play detective, we must be certain Simon never knows your connection with all this. I suspect these chaps are not playing games, you know."

I shuddered. "Yes, I do know. Andrew will be here tomorrow. Let's ask him. He may think of something."

13

The next morning, I breakfasted early and was dressed and ready to drive to London as soon as I had seen MacDougal. As it was a free day at the festival, with no performance scheduled that evening, I could run up, stay over, and bring Andrew back with me to Burling the next day.

When MacDougal arrived at the Dolphin, he assured me he needed no breakfast, having consumed quantities of coffee and buns as he drove.

Looking around the lounge area, he shook his head. "Better not talk here, Mrs. H. How about my car?"

"Or mine. I'm just off to London."

"Righto."

We walked to the car park at the back of the hotel where I settled into the driver's seat, with MacDougal next to me. Assuming his usual posture, legs apart, elbows on knees, body bent nearly double, he looked up at me sideways with a wry grin. "Now that you've become a private eye, Mrs. H., give me the full story of yesterday's caper, as you Yanks would say."

I looked around to be sure we were alone, then speaking in a low voice, I gave him every detail I could remember while he took notes, asking a question now and then.

When I had finished, he looked back at his notes. "Right. Out the London Road, just before the crest of a hill, turn right on a rough lane. About a five-minute walk's distance into the woods. Down in a hollow, metal box by a tree, covered with branches. Should be a breeze to find, if you know where to look."

"I've been wondering about drugs, Mr. MacDougal. We know Julian Kingsley was pretty heavily into cocaine. Maybe there's a connection here."

"I hope we'll know more about that when I pry open one of those crates. By the bye, I thought I had a lead in town yesterday. I popped into the office of your friend's City Freight Services—a dingy little place on the south side of the river—and overheard a driver chap come in and ask for his pay packet. I followed him out to a pub and had no trouble getting him to chat about where he makes pickups and deliveries, and that. Only I didn't learn a thing. He's been with the firm for a month and has only made local runs in London."

"I suppose they must have some legitimate business for cover."

"So it seems. Then I tried to speak with your Mrs. Veeda Riley. I tracked her down in one of her record shops and didn't get the time o' day from her. You may have better luck with her yourself, Mrs. H."

"Actually, I had planned to look her up this afternoon. Did you tell her you were working for us?"

"No, I'd only do that with your permission. I was a motorcar salesman, and my former client, Mr. Julian Kingsley, had given me a lead before his untimely death. She said she was satisfied with her current model, and thank you very much. A nice looking lady, that, but no nonsense about her."

I laughed. "A detective's lot is not always a happy one, I take it."

"Only in the films, Mrs. H., and that's a fact. I expect better things today. I've some matters to look into here in Burling, but first I'll twitch my mantle blue and it's off to the woods, if not the pastures!"

Milton again! I gazed fondly at MacDougal's retreating back, glad that he was on the job for us.

By eleven o'clock that morning, I was back in our London flat, ringing up Veeda Riley. I had listed the numbers of all four of her shops and caught her on the second try.

When I had identified myself, her voice was guarded. "Yes, of course, I remember you very well."

"I'd like to talk with you again, if I may."

No reply. I could hear voices and the tapping of a typewriter. At last I said, "Mrs. Riley—?"

The throaty voice now came through, low but decisive. "Yes, all right. I'm knocking off early today. Come round to the flat about half-past four, if you like."

Scarcely waiting for my "Thank you," she rang off.

At my desk in the study, I picked up the typescript of the book I was working on with Andrew. During the time of the Southmere Festival, I had put it aside, but now that he was in London for the week, we would have a chance to talk over some of the technical problems that inevitably arise in a collaboration.

Although Andrew, as a distinguished professor of music with an impressive record of publication, was the "name" author and I was second banana, he had generously split the publisher's advance money with me. When the subject of our biography, the wealthy owner of a talent agency with some of the most renowned clients in the music world, had died under mysterious circumstances, Andrew had offered to withdraw, but the editor had aptly, if ghoulishly, pointed out that his death wouldn't hurt the sales. Having divided up the list of celebrities, each of us had been able to use the advance to travel to some pretty exciting places to interview our subject's rich and famous clients.

Now I looked over the material I had written, planning to spend half an hour on revisions, and discovering, inevitably, that two hours had gone by.

Nearly one o'clock—lunch time in England. I rang up James's office and learned that he expected to return from court before going to lunch.

"Tell him I'm coming in, please!"

I snatched up coat and gloves and set off on the short walk to the grounds of Grays Inn, with its jewel-green lawns and magnificent old trees. The day was cold, but no rain fell as yet from the darkening sky.

As I entered the small waiting room of the offices of Hall, Dexter, Smith, and Hall, the receptionist slid back the glass panel and smiled at me. "Good afternoon, Mrs. Hall. I'm afraid Mr. Hall hasn't returned yet. Would you care to wait in his office?"

"Yes, thank you."

I was about to step through into the passage when a woman I had noticed sitting in the corner stood up. "Excuse me, ma'am. You're Mrs. 'all, are you? Can I speak to you, please?"

Middle-aged, clutching an old tweed coat around her ample middle, the woman glanced at the receptionist's head visible through the glass and took me by the arm. "Out here, then, if you don't mind."

Giving me no chance to object, she bundled me down the passage and out to the walk.

"Bit of fresh air feels good," she announced, not noticing that I had just come in from the cold.

"I'm Mrs. 'awks, Dan's mum. I was waiting for your 'usband, see, but I can't wait all day, so I'll tell you what I found out."

"Please, Mrs. Hawks," I protested, "I have nothing to do—"

"Never you mind, now. Here's what 'appened. I sent young Bill—that Dan's brother, he's fourteen—along to that there gunsmith shop to talk to the boy as seen the robbers that night what shot 'is dad, and Tommy—that's the boy—says he saw the sneakers as the tall one was wearing and they was white with a sort of X on the side like it was inked on."

"But Mrs. Hawks, please wait for Mr. Hall—"

Pulling her wool cap down over her ears with work-roughened hands, Mrs. Hawks took no notice. "Now our Dan's never had sneakers with no X on 'em. So you see it couldn't have been Dan, now, could it? He's been in trouble, true enough. I ought to've belted 'im more when he was a young'n, but I'm that soft—"

She looked hard as nails to me but I made no further effort to stem the flow.

"Now you just tell Mr. 'all what I told you. He's ever so kind, and now he can get our Dan in the clear. Time I was off!"

I watched as she went down the walk, then gratefully retreated to James's office, where a fire had been laid. I soon had it going and was warming my feet on the fender when James arrived and kissed me.

"Darling! I was hoping you'd come in. Two phone calls and we'll be off to lunch." Glancing at his messages, James frowned. "Bad news, I'm afraid. Here's a message from MacDougal: 'The magpie has been to the nest. Everything gone. Will ring you later.' "

"Oh, no! I was so sure we would get the answer to

what was in those crates. They must have been re-
moved in the night."

"Or early this morning."

Over a bowl of soup and a bottle of wine, I told
James about my encounter with Mrs. Hawks.

"But James," I concluded, "could Tommy actually
see that much in the dark?"

"It's possible. White shoes would shine out in the
dark, I expect. I've looked over the shop, and there is
only a short flight of stairs to the landing where
Tommy and Mrs. Wilkins were standing. The police
haven't told me about the X Tommy claims to have
seen. They may be saving that for a surprise."

"But if Dan Hawks never owned a pair of shoes
marked like that?"

"I'm afraid the word of his mother and all of his
friends wouldn't be worth much in court, especially
with the kind of company he keeps. But if he had worn
such a pair on the night of the shooting, he would have
tossed them out in the rubbish before now. I'll wager
the police are questioning other acquaintances to find
someone who will testify that Dan did wear sneakers
of that description. If they don't find one, unfortunately it proves nothing. It's impossible to prove one
didn't have a given item."

"Yes, I see. I'm afraid Mrs. Hawks believes this will
get her Dan off the hook."

"Certainly not now, it won't. If we go to trial, the
barrister who tries the case may wish to use it. We'll
see."

Then we talked about the significance of learning
that Simon was evidently involved in something illegal
with the man Corcoran.

James said, "It puts a different light on Riccardo's
gossip about the quarrel between Julian and Simon. If

Julian was getting close to discovering serious criminal activity on Simon's part—?''

"Yes, I know. It's just that it's hard to see Simon in the role of murderer, isn't it? He's so sort of—''

"Feckless?''

"Yes, exactly. But I suppose killers do come in all types and shapes. I only hope it's not true. It would be so awful for Bettina.''

I told James about my appointment with Veeda Riley at half-past four that afternoon. "I'm sure she knows something, or why would she let me come to see her again?''

"Yes, it sounds encouraging. Also, Andrew's coming to the flat at seven. He insists on taking us out to dine.''

"Oh, marvelous. I should be back before he arrives.''

I decided to take the tube to Kilburn, as driving in late afternoon traffic was horrendous. From Holborn, I changed at Tottenham Court Road to the northern line and reached the Kilburn station with plenty of time to walk to number 20 Gorston Road.

Veedy Riley let me in and gestured to the sofa where I had sat before, while she sank into her low chair, gathering a green velvet negligee around her knees.

I hadn't expected tea, and I was right. The sherry bottle stood between us on the coffee table.

"Have a sherry, luv.''

I poured from the half-empty bottle, suspecting that Veeda was not on her first drink of the afternoon.

"It's good of you to see me,'' I began noncommittally.

She let a silence fall between us, then looked at me, her violet eyes smoldering.

"They haven't arrested your husband, have they?''

"No, not yet, but he seems to be their prime suspect. No one else appears to have both the opportunity and the motive—as they see it—to kill Julian. If they find even a shred of evidence against him, they'll be down on him in a flash."

"I see." Again that pondering silence.

Then, "I don't suppose the bitch has recanted?"

"I spoke to her only yesterday and got nowhere."

"Look here, Jane. I've thought about this a good deal since you were here the other day. If I tell you something in strictest confidence, can I can trust you?"

"Yes."

"Right, then. I happen to know there are people who had good reason, as they saw it, to put Julian out of the way. I can't tell you who they are, or what they are up to, but I've decided this much. If your husband is arrested for this crime, I'll give you enough information to at least spread the suspicion in another direction, away from your James. Only you must never reveal that it came from me. It could be dangerous, you understand?"

"Yes, I understand."

I waited quietly, knowing that gushing gratitude would only offend this courageous lady.

"Of course you wonder why I would do this. Not merely for principles of justice, luv, although I wouldn't want to see an innocent man accused of murder. You see, if the people I refer to did have anything to do with Julian's death, then whatever loyalty I may have felt in the past—well, you see what I mean?"

"Yes, I do."

She stood up. "Then give me a ring if—if it comes to that."

I finished off my sherry and, rising from the sofa, I simply put my arms around her and felt the warmth of her embrace. What a fool Julian had been, I thought, to give up Veeda Riley for Margot.

As I started down the stairs, I heard footsteps coming up and passed a short, slight man in jeans and an anorak, his head bent, his left arm wrapped around his body in an odd posture. He scarcely glanced at me, breathing heavily as he climbed.

At the next landing, I saw a splotch of bright red on the bare wood. Paint? I looked up, but it was plain that no paint of any color, least of all red, had touched those dingy walls for a long time. A few steps farther down, another splash of red appeared, then every few steps a drop of reddish brown, growing browner as I descended.

Blood! The man must have been injured. And he was certainly headed for Veeda's flat, as he had passed the landing on the middle floor before our paths crossed.

On an impulse, I clattered noisily down the remaining stairs, slammed the outer door while standing inside, then slipped off my shoes and began to climb, stepping on the side of the treads nearest the wall to avoid creaks and squeaks.

As I reached the steps below the top floor landing, I heard the man's voice crying out hoarsely, "Veeda, let me in! Be quick, for God's sake!" and the sound of locks being released.

Then the door opened and Veeda's voice, "Riley! What's the trouble?"

The man obviously pushed past her into the flat and the door slammed shut.

Without a second thought, I climbed the remaining stairs, crept along the wall, and put my ear to the door, surprised at how clearly I could hear the voices inside.

Veeda was saying, "Here's the towel. Press it tight, that's it. Now, Riley, what happened?"

"Never you mind what happened. I'm hurt, that's enough."

"I'm fed up with you and your goings on. This is the last time I help you, and that's flat."

"Sure and I've heard that tale before, Veeda. You want to see your precious brother in the nick, is that it?"

"All right, then. Come to the sink where I can deal with that arm."

And the voices moved out of range.

115

14

I was still in the bath when Andrew arrived at our flat that evening. When I finally emerged, dressed for dining out, I found James and Andrew cozily chatting over a whisky.

Long ago, after I had finished my degree, Andrew and I had made the transition from professor and graduate student to friends of equal standing. Now, as we embraced, I looked into Andrew's fine and sensitive face and saw his smile of pleasure.

"Jane! You're looking marvelous!"

"And you, too. Even a suntan!"

"Yes. It was in the seventies when I left Los Angeles."

James handed me a drink, smiling. "Some day we'll join the set that dashes off to the Riviera in the winter. Jane will simply have to suffer through meanwhile."

I looked into James's clear blue eyes and laughed. "Andrew can see how I suffer! But tell me, how did you get away in October, even for a week?"

"When I was asked to give a talk at the conference in London, I checked it out with dear Martha, who said to put my seminar on assignment and go! She's talking of giving up the department chair next year."

"Oh, no!"

"Yes. God help us if we get Bradshaw—"

When we had exhausted our usual spate of shoptalk, Andrew asked James what was new in his line, and James gave him an account of the Dan Hawks case, while I added the story of my encounter with Dan's mother that afternoon.

"It's hard to know whether or not to believe her story that Dan never owned a pair of white sneakers marked with an *X*. She would obviously lie through her teeth to protect her Dan, but somehow I found her indignation convincing."

James said, "I agree. If Dan had tossed away a pair of incriminating shoes, they would all have shut up like clams on the whole subject. After lunch this afternoon, Jane, I had the unhappy task of ringing up Mrs. Hawks and giving her the news that neither the police nor the magistrate is likely to dismiss the case on the grounds of Dan's *not* owning said sneakers, and I was greeted with some pretty colorful language from Mum!"

When we had finished our drinks, we set off for the French restaurant Andrew favored, and over three exquisite courses, James and I gave Andrew the full story of Julian Kingsley's death and its attendant details.

Speculating about that afternoon's encounter with Veeda Riley's bleeding visitor, we agreed that what I had overheard about a brother and his involvement with Riley did constitute some sort of motive for murdering Julian Kingsley.

"They knew she would inherit a packet of money from Julian," James said, "and evidently planned to relieve her of a fair share of it."

"Yes," Andrew pondered. "Or Julian may have been involved in some way in their activities, and they rubbed him out."

"On the other hand," I put in, "the killer may be someone at Southmere. You'll meet all the principals tomorrow, Andrew. In any case, we're counting on you to do your Sherlock Holmes bit."

And James added, "We may be too close to the case to see it. What we need is a view from the bridge."

The next morning, I picked up Andrew at the friend's flat where he usually stayed on his visits to London, bringing along the typescript of my portion of our book and using the time on the drive to Sussex to iron out all sorts of details.

Reading through my work, he said, "I like your colloquial style, Jane. It strikes the right note for our readership, I think. We want accuracy but not academic pedantry."

Then we spoke of mutual friends in Los Angeles. I asked about my friend Ellen, whom Andrew had met in the summer.

"We're the best of friends. Ellen is gradually recovering from her divorce, but not yet ready—"

"For a new relationship?"

"Yes. And I'm not sure I'm ready either, Jane." Now the old familiar expression of pain, patiently endured, crossed Andrew's face at the reminder of the untimely death of his young wife a few short years before. "Ellen and I both need time."

"I understand."

At the Dolphin in Burling, where I had booked a room for Andrew for the two nights of his stay, he stashed his bag before joining me for an introductory tour of the town, which he had not visited before. Officially free for the day from my duties at Southmere, I lead Andrew on much the same circuit James and I had followed the week before, enjoying his delight in the charm of the town.

At last, we detoured into a small side street to the antique shop where James had bought my ring.

I was cordially greeted by Mrs. Lacey, the owner of the shop. "Oh, Mrs. Hall, your ring is here! It came in this morning."

The fit was perfect, and Andrew expressed his admiration for James's gift. As we turned to go, the lady of the shop asked after my friend, Mrs. Smith.

"Do you mean Mrs. Kingsley?"

"No, indeed. The pretty fair-haired lady with the young gentleman who bought the sapphire and diamond ring for her. Such a lovely couple, they were, and so happy together!"

I blinked, then smiling blandly and saying, "Yes, of course," I strolled off with Andrew.

"What was all that about?" he asked with a smile.

I told him about seeing Margot as she left the shop one day, and the appearance of a sapphire and diamond ring on her hand. "But Andrew, what would you say is the age of the lady in the shop?"

"Oh, in her forties, I'd guess."

"Exactly. Julian was forty-seven when he died. To a lady in her seventies, for example, he might appear to be 'young,' but would a lady of the same age be likely to refer to him as 'a young gentleman'? I doubt it."

"Yes, I see. So who was the happy young Mr. Smith who bought Margot a ring?"

"That's an extremely interesting question."

Before leaving the Dolphin, I had rung up Bettina and asked her for lunch to meet Andrew, reluctantly including Simon in the invitation and glad to learn that he was out.

"But may I bring Russell?" Bettina had asked. "He's been an angel this morning, helping with the usual headaches!"

Accordingly, Andrew and I secured a table for four at The Bell, a pleasant little restaurant off the High Street, and ten minutes into the lunch, the four of us were chatting like old friends. Russell Ames, his eyes looking mock serious through his dark-rimmed glasses, told amusing tales of conducting orchestras in bizarre circumstances. Andrew contributed incidents from academia. Inevitably the three of us regaled Andrew with Anton Szabo stories.

Her laughter subsiding, Bettina said, "Anton *is* dedicated, at least. One must grant him that."

Only Bettina could make a Pollyanna remark like that and manage to look captivating. I could see Andrew falling under her innocent spell and joining Russell in the Bettina fan club.

Back at the Dolphin, I looked into the small lounge, where Ilena and Dmitri were absorbed in a game of gin rummy, both of them humming softly as they played, in that maddening habit of singers warming up on the day of a performance. Raymond sat on a sofa near the window, reading a current issue of the *Journal of Psychiatry*.

When I introduced Andrew, the four of us who were either past or present residents of Los Angeles ran through the usual clichés about the weather. Then Raymond and Andrew discovered a mutual acquaintance from the university, while Dmitri remarked, "I have been to the East Coast of the United States but never to the West. I hope to be there one day, if my agent will find me something there, yes?" He looked at Ilena with soulful dark eyes.

Raymond beamed. "Yes, good idea. We can put you up, if we're at home, right, Ilena?"

Ilena looked down at her cards. "Of course, if you wish it."

I smiled. "You have to be away from home a good deal, don't you, Ilena? I notice you have some excellent bookings coming up."

Raymond answered for her. "Yes. Her career is moving along very well. We can turn down some of the lesser offers now, since I can't always get away."

I had often wondered how Raymond managed to leave his practice, but I didn't think it was up to me to ask him.

Now he gestured to the journal in his hand. "I was just reading an article on ambivalence in male-female relationships. This guy says that in its extreme form it may lead to violence, even murder, if it remains untreated. Either the man or the woman may have powerful feelings of both love and hate for the spouse or partner, especially in a committed relationship."

Andrew asked, "Is the violence usually directed at the object of the ambivalence?"

"Often it is, yes. But he cites cases where the violence is committed against an outside person." Giving us a few examples from the article, Raymond massaged his beard, his face beaming with astonished joy.

I noticed that Ilena and Dmitri had resumed their game. Humming away and totally absorbed, they seemed to hear nothing of what was being said, and again I was reminded of children playing while the grownups conversed.

*   *   *

As we left the small lounge, Andrew murmured his delight in the dark wood panelling and low-beamed ceilings of the inn, much of it unchanged since the fifteenth century.

"You must see the bar," I said, leading the way down a passage, over uneven floors, into a panelled room with multi-colored lights winking through the diamond panes of the windows.

"Jane!" Riccardo leapt to his feet from a deep chair before the enormous fireplace, clutching what looked like a brandy.

When I presented Andrew, Riccardo insisted we join him.

"We've had wine with lunch, Riccardo," I protested.

"Then Perrier?"

Agreeing, we settled before the fire and Riccardo burst out with his tale of woe.

"Jane, my darling, it is dreadful! I asked for you when I come into the hotel and they said you are out. How happy I am to see you. I have been questioned by the police!"

"Yes, Riccardo," I replied patiently. "All of us have been questioned since Julian's death."

"Ah, yes, but this is about the man in the burning house."

At Andrew's questioning look, Riccardo, thrilled to have a new listener, gave him the much-embroidered story of my heroism on the day of the fire.

"But now the police found out I saw the man, and they asked me to come into the station to describe him, except I do not remember much. He was about the same height as me—five feet ten inches."

Andrew and I exchanged an amused glance at Riccardo's blandly adding at least two inches to his height.

"His hair was light color and wavy. That is all I know. They ask me over and over if the man has an accent, but I say, I am Italian, how do I know about the accent in English?"

"How did the police find out that you had seen the man, Riccardo?"

"It is the man at the garage, who repaired my car. I am so upset at the time, I tell him about making the phone call from the old house, and the word—how you say?—goes around in a small town like Burling."

"Well," I said with a smile, "I see they didn't lock you up."

Riccardo's dark eyes gazed into mine. "Do not make the joke, my angel. One never knows with the police, eh? They may come in middle of the night and take me away!"

15

Half an hour later, Andrew and I arrived at South-mere, where I gave him the obligatory tour of the old stone tower. Standing on the terrace, he shook his head.

"I see why no one believes Kingsley's fall was an accident, Jane. A man would have to climb up onto this balustrade, or at least swing one leg over and push himself off. Suicide, yes. Accident? Not likely. And Kingsley certainly doesn't sound like a candidate to end his life in the midst of the festival!"

"Exactly. The blow on the head which the medical examiner thinks could not have been caused by the fall makes it pretty clear it was murder."

Back on the ground floor of the tower, I put the torch in its usual place and lead the way down the hill to the theater where Andrew carefully studied the layout, both backstage and front.

"Exactly where were you sitting at the beginning of the rehearsal?" he asked.

"About here." I walked toward a seat on the center aisle, ten or twelve rows from the front.

Sitting in the seat I indicated, Andrew looked up

and back to the curve of boxes. "If you had looked up there, you could have seen our friend the psychiatrist."

"Yes, but evidently I didn't look that way."

Now Andrew looked to his right at the front box on the second tier. "You could see Margot and her husband from here, of course?"

"Yes. Margot was on this side, with Julian on her right, behind the plush drape. He liked to watch the stage rehearsals from there. I noticed he sat in the same place at the orchestra run-through."

"But how could he see the stage?"

"He must have pulled the drape aside. Let's go up and see."

In the Kingsley box, Andrew took the chair on the right, while I sat in Margot's chair.

"Simple enough," he said. "Look here, it's probably hanging just as it was that evening."

Instead of being pulled across to the side wall of the box, the small curtain hung several inches free, leaving ample space for Julian to see the action on the stage. Going back out the door behind Julian's chair, we followed the curving passage, stopping at the box at the first bend where Andrew opened the door.

"This must be where Raymond was sitting."

"Yes, I should think he was just about here."

"Notice that the interior of the theater is not actually a U shape—more of a shallow U, open at the ends. So, the doctor, if this is where he sat, is looking directly down the same side as the Kingsley box. The occupants would be more or less out of his sight."

"Yes, but Margot could have seen Raymond if she had leaned forward and looked back this way."

"The police may already have asked her that, Jane. I wonder what she said."

I laughed bitterly. "Her word isn't worth much, but I'm sure Raymond will ask her the same thing."

On the way down, we stopped at the lighting booth under the second tier where Andrew admired the up-to-date equipment. Sitting in the chair of the lights technician, he gazed out toward the stage. "Let's see what can be seen from here."

"And here," I added, taking the chair of the assistant to his left.

"The Kingsley box itself is visible, but you'd have to make a special effort to see the interior, especially with the house dark for dress rehearsal."

"Yes. And Anton keeps these fellows fairly busy. He does a lot with changing effects, which I have to admit are often good, but I imagine the technicians have to watch their cue sheets pretty carefully."

Andrew peered to his right. "Can't see the doctor's box at all from here, of course, as it's above us."

"That's right. Not much help here, I'm afraid."

When we had descended to the foyer and walked through to the wings, Andrew stood in the spot I indicated, from where I had watched the rehearsal.

"What was happening in the opera at this point, Jane?"

"Let's see. Alfredo and Violetta have their long chat about love. Then she gives him the flower and he leaves. Then the chorus comes in at that point and they all start saying good night to Violetta."

"Yes. So, this must be about five minutes to seven?"

"I should think so. It was at this point that Anton Szabo stopped the performance to harangue the chorus as they were departing. Poor Russell was looking extremely irritated. He had tried to tell Anton it's not customary to have interruptions during a dress rehearsal, but to no avail. The chorus trooped back on and went out again, trying to act like guests leaving a party, and not, as Anton complained, a flock of sheep rushing to the feeding pen.''

"All right. Dmitri Mikos—as Alfredo—presumably has gone to his dressing room, as he has a short break until the end of the act. So where is everyone else?''

"Well, the chorus are all in the green room; Riccardo is in his dressing room, no doubt humming and warming; Simon is at the main house, dressing; Russell Ames and the orchestra are in the pit; the Kingsleys are in their box, Raymond's in *his* box, and all's right with the world.''

"Then Violetta is alone on stage, doing her big aria. Shortly before seven, just at the momentary break, everyone hears Margot tell Julian to go, and Anton is standing under the Kingsley box?''

"Yes, then after '*Sempre libera*,' Alfredo is heard offstage, and the duet ends the act.''

"About ten minutes past seven, then. You know, Jane, the timing is remarkably close. Julian leaves here, arrives at the tower two minutes later, climbs the stairs to his rendezvous—another two minutes. He's struck on the head and pitched over. Say, two or three minutes past seven. James arrives about five minutes later, sees Julian, sprints to the stage door and phones for an ambulance at eleven minutes after seven. He might easily have seen the killer leave the tower if he had been minutes earlier.''

"I only wish he had!''

"At any rate, it's clear that no one engaged in the rehearsal of the first act could have done the deed.''

I lowered my voice. "You know, Andrew, ever since we learned at the antique shop this morning that Margot may have a lover, I've realized that she had a powerful motive for disposing of Julian—all that money, and the young 'Mr. Smith' to boot. We know she couldn't have done it herself, but what if she *hired* someone to kill Julian?"

"Or more simply, what if the mysterious Mr. Smith did it for both of them?"

"Yes, except that when they tried to ride off together into the sunset, the police might cast a jaundiced eye on the happy young man."

"She's kept his identity in the dark so far, Jane. Perhaps they will pretend to have met after Julian's death."

"Then they shouldn't have paraded around Burling buying rings and looking happy!"

Andrew laughed, and we made our way down to the foyer and into Bettina's office, to ask if she needed some help.

Her huge eyes merry, Bettina said, "You won't believe this, darlings, but all is quiet. I'm thinking of leaving the staff in charge and going over to the house for a rest."

Inevitably, the phone rang. Smiling, Bettina reached for the receiver. "I'll take this one, and then go."

Andrew picked up one of the jade monkeys on Bettina's desk, idly turning it in his hands. "See No Evil," he mused. "Good advice, if the world would cooperate."

Now Bettina's face had clouded. "Yes, dear, I'll be there directly."

Putting the phone down, she reached for her coat. "It's Simon. He wants me to come to the house."

As we drove back to the Dolphin, rain began to fall, driven by a gusty wind that made the air feel miserably cold.

Andrew said, "I hope nothing was wrong. Bettina seemed concerned when her husband called."

"It may be nothing serious. Simon is capable of making a fuss about trifles."

"Mmm. You know, Jane, Bettina reminds me of Norma."

I caught my breath at this rare mention of the charming young wife Andrew had lost. Saying nothing, I put my hand briefly on his arm, then drove on in silence to the car park of the Dolphin.

Pushing against the icy, wind-swept rain, we dashed for the shelter of the inn, in time for a restorative pot of tea in the lounge.

An hour and a half later, we were on our way back to Southmere for the evening performance of *Traviata*, swathed in warm gear over our evening clothes against what now promised to be a full-fledged storm.

Musically, the performance of *Traviata* was again a resounding success, the young singers settling into their roles with confidence. I was always intrigued with the way performers shed their everyday personalities. Ilena, who often behaved like a sulky child, became a sophisticated, slightly world-weary Violetta, carrying the difficult role with aplomb. Gossipy and emotional Riccardo emerged as the elderly, dignified Germont. Only Dmitri, whose Alfredo demanded little beyond good singing and looking handsome, had less to change from his real-life persona.

Andrew shook his head over Anton Szabo's bizarre staging. "I suppose in time this trend will run its course, Jane. Meanwhile, audiences seem to passively accept whatever they are given, if they want to hear the opera!"

At the second interval, Anton turned up in the central foyer where I introduced him to Andrew.

"Oh, yes, the professor from California, right?" Anton described his invitation to do a seminar at the university and listened with some interest to Andrew's account of the people involved.

129

Then, running a hand through his black curly hair, he eyed Andrew challengingly. "So what do you think of the staging for tonight's show?"

Andrew smiled. "I can't say I like it much. I prefer my Verdi straight up, so to speak."

Anton's black eyes glittered. "Great! I like a frank opinion. Little Jane, here, is full of tact and diplomacy."

Surprised at his perception, I laughed. "After all, Anton, I'm a paid employee at the moment. Catch me when I'm off the payroll."

After the last of the curtain calls from the enthusiastic audience, we went backstage to Ilena's dressing room to join the small crowd of well-wishers. Removing the chalk-white makeup of the dying Violetta, Ilena thanked Andrew for the flowers he had arranged to have sent to her. Raymond, beaming as always, stood behind her, one hand on her shoulder, as she received her visitors.

"We'll see you onstage," I said, as we turned to go.

Margot had surprised everyone by ordering a buffet table of sandwiches and wine to be served onstage after the performance that evening.

Bettina had explained, "Margot wants to begin seeing people again, and this seemed a good way to start. She's been shut up in the house the entire week, poor darling. She'll come to the theater after the performance."

And as we walked onstage, there indeed was Margot, standing by the loaded table, looking gorgeous in pants and sweater, talking animatedly to Russell Ames.

16

When I presented Andrew to Margot, she gave him an appraising look. "I see that all professors are not owls."

Andrew smiled "If that's a compliment, I thank you."

Margot's voice was sultry. "It is indeed."

Although her words sounded vaguely flirtatious, I could see that Margot's mind was not really on Andrew. Her eyes flickered about as if she were looking for someone.

Russell Ames obligingly intervened with a question about the weather. "Was the storm subsiding as you came across, Margot?"

She frowned. "No, actually it's blowing up very badly. I was nearly swept off my feet coming through the garden."

I asked, "Were you here at Southmere during the hurricane two years ago?"

And as others came up to greet Margot, everyone exchanged tales of the infamous storm that had swept across southern England, causing not only extensive damage but injuries and even death. While London and other regions had been badly hit, the south coast had recieved the brunt of the storm.

Margot described some of the damage at South-mere. "The house was fairly untouched, except that bits of the roof were ripped away, but the gardens were a shambles, and dozens of trees were down. Julian was most upset."

At the mention of Julian's name, faces sobered while voices eagerly filled what might have been an awkward silence.

As Bettina and Simon approached, the group around Margot shifted, and soon she was surrounded by peo-ple balancing plates and glasses of wine while they chatted amiably. Anton Szabo strolled in, saw Margot, marched straight through the crowd to shake her hand, then retreated to the buffet table.

"Dutifully paying his respects to the châtelaine," I murmured to Andrew.

When Ilcna finally made her entrance, on Ray-mond's arm, everyone broke into applause for the prima donna and raised their glasses in a toast, grace-fully delivered by Russell Ames.

While there would be a proper cast party on the closing night of each opera, this occasion made a pleasant interim, with members of the small chorus joining the festivities until their van arrived to deliver them to their destination.

I saw Riccardo bidding good night to his lady friend, and when she had gone with the others, I said with a smile, "Your friend is not staying this evening?"

Unabashed, he gazed at me with liquid dark eyes. "Ah, no. I am too fatigued after the performance. You understand?" I understood.

Now I joined Andrew as he stood with a convivial group. Simon was telling an amusing anecdote from his university days, while Bettina gazed adoringly. As the laughter and conversation went on, I said to Bettina, "Was everything all right with Simon this afternoon?"

She looked puzzled.

"When he rang you up in your office and asked you to come over to the house?"

Her face cleared, her eyes merry. "Oh, yes, he was looking for a certain pair of socks. I found them for him!"

Repressing any comment, I merely said, "I'm glad everything was all right."

Now a small frown appeared. "Actually, Jane, I'm a bit worried about Simon—"

"Bettina!"

Her master's voice brought back her smile, as Simon asked her to recall some detail for the story he was about to relate.

Presently, people began to leave, heavily bundled against the storm. Riccardo had said his thanks to Margot and gone, but three minutes later he was back eyes bulging, arms waving.

"Jane, my darling, I cannot drive in this frightful storm. I am terrified!"

"That's all right, Riccardo. You can come with us."

"Ah, but I wish to have my car in the morning."

Riccardo turned pleading eyes on Andrew. "*Signor,* can you drive my car, perhaps?"

"Of course, Andrew," I said. "Go ahead. I'll be fine."

"Ah, a thousand thanks, my angel!" Riccardo kissed me fervently and went off with Andrew.

When the others had gone, Simon and Margot stood together on the stage while I spent a few minutes in her office with Bettina, checking some details for the next day.

Now, as Simon approached, Bettina said softly, "I do want to talk to you, Jane. Tomorrow."

"Yes, tomorrow."

And the three of them went out toward the house.

Leaving my evening shoes in the theater, I pulled on my leather boots, tucked up my long skirt, and bundled into my warm gear against the cold. Going out on the opposite side of the theater, I saw that my car was the only one left in the car park. The wind was so strong I had to push with all my strength against it and still found it difficult to make headway.

Although I had come to the theater early, I had followed the policy that staff members should park on the far side of the area, leaving the nearer spaces for the patrons of the opera. When I opened the door, the roar of the storm was deafening, and as the wind gusted, the rain flew horizontally, cutting into my face with icy needles.

I remembered seeing on television, in the aftermath of the hurricane two years earlier, a demonstration of a man in a wind tunnel, simulating the effects of various speeds of wind. During that storm, I had been safely tucked away in my room in London and had slept through the whole thing.

Now I experienced the incredible force of those winds, coming in gusts, with intervals of lesser pressure during which I gained a few yards, then whipping up blasts which nearly lifted me off my feet. Coming from the southeast, the storm blew straight across the car park and up toward the tower, while my car was down to my left, directly in the path of the wind.

When at last I reached the perimeter of the asphalt, where it bordered a grove of trees below the tower, I slipped and fell, getting a nasty knock on my left knee.

Trying to regain my feet, I looked up, and what I saw filled me with horror. An enormous beech tree, perhaps twenty feet away, was swaying ominously, and then, in a slow arc, its great branches began to descend toward the spot where I lay.

Desperately, I scrabbled uphill on hands and knees, away from the falling tree, this time aided by the wind, which pushed me along like a helpful friend. The roar of the storm was so deafening that I thought no other sound could be heard, but when that great beech fell, the ground shook, and a sepulchral moan issued from its carcass.

I thought I had crept out of the danger zone, but the end of a branch near the top of the tree had caught me across the legs and I found myself pinned to the ground. A spray of beech leaves lay gently over my face like a wreath, their pungent scent filling my nostrils.

Carefully, I moved one leg, then the other, and was mollified to learn that evidently there were no broken bones.

Now the wind helped again, for as it gusted, the tree rocked from side to side, allowing the branch to lift ever so slightly. With each opportunity, I wriggled a few inches closer to deliverance, finally getting both legs free.

When at last I struggled to my feet, bruised but unbowed, the wind pushed me up toward the tower, and I was too exhausted to resist. Stumbling through the heavy wooden door, I groped for the torch and switched it on, closing the door behind me. I could ask for nothing better than to shelter here until the storm subsided.

As I flashed the light from the torch over the assorted relics, no doubt stored here and forgotten, my heart leaped up when I saw the high back of a sofa which faced the far wall. Picking my way through the debris, I threw myself down on the worn upholstery, glad that I had found a better bed than the cold stone floor. High up on the walls on either side, two barred slits, open to the elements, would give me a clue to the condition of the storm, also providing a faint light, as I learned when I stretched out and switched off the torch.

How long it was, I couldn't be sure—perhaps half an hour—until I emerged from a half doze and realized that the sounds from outside had lowered by a good many decibels. The splatters of rain had already ceased coming through the aperture above me, and now the sliver of light was perceptibly brighter. Moonlight?

Time to go. Just as I forced my protesting body to move, I heard the unmistakable sounds of a car stopping and footsteps approaching the door of the tower. Ready to welcome a fellow refugee from the storm, I sat up and prepared to switch on the torch when the door opened and closed and I heard Margot's voice.

"Darling! Hold me, hold me once more before I go!"

It didn't take me long to realize that if I kept quiet, I was about to learn who Margot's mystery lover was. With no qualms at all about eavesdropping, I sank back, securely hidden by the high back of the sofa. Even if a light was flashed my way, I knew I could not be seen.

I heard the man murmur, then Margot's voice again, but one I could scarcely identify with the Margot I knew. Humble and pleading, she was saying, "You *do* love me, don't you? Just tell me again!"

The man evidently produced an "I love you," although I could not distinguish the words.

Then after a pause, Margot moaned, "I can't bear this a moment longer. Every day without you is an eternity. On Tuesday night, when you didn't come to the meeting place, I walked up and down the road, up and down—I thought I would go mad. And you were asleep! How could you?"

Another murmur from the man, while I thought: Tuesday night? That's why Margot looked so haggard and depressed on Wednesday when I saw her in Bettina's office.

Now Margot cried out, "Don't you see, darling, I want to be with you night and day, not in stolen moments."

Another murmur.

Margot's voice was quavery, edgy with tears. "I know, darling. When Julian was alive, it had to be. He would never have let me go. But now it's different. Kiss me again, my sweet."

Long pause.

"Tomorrow night?"

Much as I longed to sit up and try to get a glimpse of the man, I knew it was too dark to identify anyone, and I dared not risk exposure.

I heard the door to the tower open and close. Then Margot's footsteps went off down the hill, and I heard the car drive away.

I waited until I was sure they were gone. Then at last I stumbled down the hill to my car. The night was as quiescent as if the storm had never happened, and the moon smiled innocently on the landscape.

I saw that my beech was not the only tree downed by the wind, but the damage was minimal compared with that of the storm two years before.

As I reached the bottom of the hill, I saw a car

parked in the deep shadows formed by the wall of the Italian garden. No doubt someone had left the car and gone home with a friend.

When I finally reached my room at the Dolphin, I tossed my wet, muddy clothes into the tub and crawled gratefully into bed.

17

Exhausted as I was after my encounter with the storm, I was too electrified by what I had learned about Margot to be anywhere near to sleep. It had been easy enough to surmise from the episode in the antique shop that Margot had a lover. Now it was no longer in doubt that Margot had a powerful motive for disposing of her husband.

Frustrated at not learning the identity of the man, I wondered if he was in fact someone totally unknown to me. Evidently, the two had been meeting at night during Margot's nocturnal walks, which Bettina had supposed were expressions of Margot's grief over her husband.

In any case, the man was clearly a prime suspect for Julian's murder. Equally possible was the theory that someone had been hired to do the deed. And, if that's how it was done, I was sure it was Margot who was behind it, both with the money and the plan. She was obviously besotted with her beloved—probably because it was the first time any man had been less than abjectly devoted to her.

Again, as I had done on earlier occasions, I faced

the possibility that my resentment of Margot warped my judgment. There were certainly other people who could have murdered Julian, perhaps for reasons we knew nothing about.

When James arrived in Burling the next day, he brought information which gave us a different angle on the case, but I was unaware of that as I lay sleepless, staring at the dark ceiling of my room at the Dolphin.

Suddenly, I heard a soft tapping at my door. Looking at the clock, I saw that it had been only about half an hour since I got back from Southmere.

Pulling on a robe, I opened the door the scant few inches permitted by the chain and saw the man who was night clerk at the inn.

"Yes, what is it?"

"I'm so sorry to disturb you, Mrs. Hall, but I have an urgent message."

"Yes?"

"I am to tell you that Mrs. Barnes wants you to meet her at once at the tower at Southmere. You are to tell no one, and on no account must you ring up the house."

Bettina! Something really dreadful must have happened for her to summon me at such an hour.

Without a moment's thought, I dressed and ran to my car, my aches and bruises forgotten as I sped back to Southmere and pulled up near the tower.

No sign of Bettina.

Pushing open the door, I called out. No answer.

There was the torch, where I had hastily replaced it less than an hour ago. With the aid of its light, I checked out the ground floor, even peering over the back of my old friend the sofa. No Bettina.

Going back near the entrance, I sat on the bottom stair to wait.

Then I heard it—a voice, calling weakly from somewhere above me. "Jane!"

"Bettina! Where are you?"

"Up here! Help me!"

Grasping the iron railing on the outer wall of the circling stairs and lighting my footsteps with the torch, I ran as quickly as I could to the first landing, again calling out her name.

Now I heard only a moaning sound, still far above.

"I'm coming, darling," I called out.

Halfway up to the second level, I heard the voice again. A groan, then faintly, "Hurry up!"

For a moment, I froze. Something was wrong, but I couldn't think what it was. Nothing to do but go on.

Now at last I emerged onto the upper level of the tower, calling out to Bettina. Only a few yards ahead of me was the terrace from which Julian had fallen to his death.

Then I heard someone breathing behind me. Before I could turn, the torch was knocked from my hand, and I felt a terrible blow on the back of my head. Afterward, I remembered the sensation of falling, but had no memory of the moment when my body struck the tower's stone floor.

Regaining consciousness was a slow process. First, I opened my eyes on what seemed complete darkness and closed them again, feeling only a desire to sleep. Then I felt a dull pain where the blow had struck my head. I heard a faint moaning sound and realized it was my own voice, floating above me like a disembodied ghost. As the pain began to throb, I was forced awake against my will, and now I felt the cold stone floor under my cheek.

Suddenly, recollection rushed back and I knew where I was and what had happened. I was lying prone, a few yards from the terrace of the tower, from which enough pale light issued to give me my bearings. Painfully trying to sit up, I pushed with my gloved right hand against the floor and found that my fist was curled over a small, hard object. Puzzled, I opened my hand to see what it was, but I could make out nothing in the dark. I shrugged and put the object in the pocket of my jeans.

Where was the torch? On hands and knees, I felt around the area where I had fallen but found nothing. Moving as sluggishly as a slow-motion film, I struggled to my feet, sweeping a larger area with my boots. Still no torch.

Then, clouds must have scudded away from the face of the moon, for a wedge of silver light illumed the segment of the tower where I stood. The torch was gone!

In my half-somnolent state, I had thought only of finding the torch and getting quickly away from the tower. Now, as my heart dealt hammer blows in my chest, I realized that my assailant might still be there.

For a moment, I stood irresolute. Should I wait and hope that help would arrive? Not very likely at this hour. It was impossible to hide in the barren tower. No, I must try to get away.

But how to get down the stairs without a light?

As I reached the top of the steps, the last finger of moonlight flickered and faded. I must make the effort now. Shuddering, I grasped the iron railing with my right hand and started down, feeling with my feet for the next step. As the total darkness enclosed me, I felt a panic so suffocating that I stopped and clung to the rail, my head against the stone wall, my breath coming in agonizing gasps.

Enough of this, I told myself sternly. One step at a

time, I worked my way down to the landing, where even the faint glimmer of light from the distant apertures gave me a respite from the strangling blackness of the stairs.

But was I alone? Waves of terror assailed me as I crossed the open area and reached the top of the last flight of stairs.

Into the darkness again, clinging to the iron rail with each painful step, I saw at last the bottom of the stairs. With a headlong rush to end this nightmare, I plunged down too rapidly, slipping before I reached the last step. My hand left the rail, and with both arms flailing, I fell, sliding down the final stairs and landing ignominiously on my back.

Again, I waited in palpitating fear for my attacker to reappear, but all was quiet.

Leaping up, I stumbled to the door, wrenched it open, ran to my car, and drove down through the car park. As I rounded the corner, I noticed that the car which had been standing by the garden wall when I left earlier had now gone.

Once safely on the road to Burling, I felt again the throbbing pain in my head which fear had suppressed. Pulling off my wool cap, I felt a swelling and a slight laceration of the scalp but nothing more.

At the Dolphin, I assured the night clerk that my friend was quite all right and asked him not to mention the incident to anyone. At last I reached my room, surprised to discover when I looked at the clock, that less than an hour had passed since I received the mysterious summons to go to Southmere.

Now, as I undressed, I found the object in my pocket that had been in my hand when I came back to consciousness after the blow. A small jade monkey, with the inscription, "Speak No Evil."

Where had I seen the monkey before? Of course. On Bettina's desk.

At eleven o'clock the next morning, I sat in bed like royalty, propped by pillows, with a tea tray on my lap, while James and Andrew, like two courtiers, listened to the tale of my night's adventure.

I had slept until almost eight o'clock, when I rang up Andrew's room to give him a cursory version of what had happened. Over my protest, he had sent for a doctor, who told me to stay down until the afternoon when he would call in again.

"I'll meet James at the train," Andrew had said. "You relax and watch television trivia. It's marvelous therapy."

In fact, the television was running a number of stories about the storm of the night before, comparing it inevitably with the hurricane in the same month, two years earlier. In both cases, the rain-softened earth had weakened the roots of trees, and in October the leaves had not yet fallen, making the trees more vulnerable to toppling over. However, last night's storm was much briefer and far less severe than its predecessor. I was interested to learn that most of the damage occurred during a final burst of high winds at precisely the time I had come out of the theater, followed by a quick abatement.

I had given this reassuring news to Andrew, who had been castigating himself for leaving me to drive back alone.

Now, as I finished the story of my peripatetic night, I laughed. "I feel such a fool, dashing back and forth like a shuttlecock."

" 'We are not amused,' " James quoted, holding my hand and looking gratifyingly solemn.

"And this time the 'we' is plural." Andrew's face was equally gloomy.

"All right, you two." I put down my teacup. "I admit I love your concern, but let's figure out who did this—and why?"

James frowned. "First, we must ask ourselves whether the person, whoever it was, actually intended to kill Jane—"

"By shoving me off the tower like Julian," I put in.

James's blue eyes were shadowed. "Or was it intended merely as a warning?"

We agreed that planting the monkey in my hand made it likely that it was a warning. I didn't add that if I *had* been pitched over the balcony, the monkey might have been put into my hand afterward, as a warning to others, perhaps.

Andrew nodded. "So, what does Jane know that could harm anyone?"

I laughed. "The most likely answer to that is the affair between Margot and her mystery lover except that neither of them has the least idea I was there and overheard them, and I never found out who he was!"

"There's Simon, of course," said James, "but he surely can't know that Jane has any information about his activities. You've never told Bettina, have you, darling?"

"No, not a word."

"Then someone may *believe* Jane knows something damaging, whether it's true or not."

Now James asked, "Assuming that the voice in the tower wasn't Bettina's—one can scarcely imagine your friend bashing you on the head—what actually did you hear?"

I frowned. "I think the first thing I heard was a voice calling my name. Of course I believed it was Bettina, since the message to come to the tower had been presumbly from her. After that, I heard a moaning sound and I thought she was hurt. Then, just before I reached the second landing, the voice sort of gasped, *'Hurry up!'* and for a moment I felt a curious stab of fear. Something said to me, 'That isn't Bettina!' I still don't know why. But of course I went on, and that's when—''

"Yes, darling." James reached for my hand again.

Andrew said, "What about the voice on the phone? Did the night clerk say whether it was a man or a woman?"

"No, he merely said he had been asked to tell me that Mrs. Barnes wanted me to meet her at the tower. I didn't stop to ask who had left the message. I simply dashed off."

"When Jane called me this morning," said Andrew, "I caught the clerk just as he was going off duty. He told me that the voice was breathless, as if the caller was in distress, but he knew nothing more."

18

When the three of us had talked over the events of the past week and confessed ourselves baffled, Andrew stood up.

"I'll leave you two now."

I leaned back on my pillows and held out a regal hand. "I feel like Elizabeth Barrett Browning, receiving from her invalid couch. All I need is the dog Flush!"

James stood up. "Shall we have lunch for three sent up here, Jane?"

"No, you two go along. I'll get some rest."

"Good idea. One o'clock in the dining room, Andrew?"

"Fine."

When Andrew had gone, James kissed me, then smiled modestly. "I've been doing some sleuthing on another angle of the case. I told Andrew about it on the way up from the train. When you first talked with Veeda Riley, she mentioned that she and her husband had been married at 'St. Ursula's,' which I took to be Church of England. We know she was living in London at the time, and I thought it likely they were married somewhere in town, so I looked up the register of parishes but found nothing.

"Then it occurred to me that the Irish names of the parties suggested the Roman Catholic church, and there I found a St. Ursula's in Marylebone. Going back to what seemed the likely years, I searched the register and presto!"

"Yes, Sherlock?"

"About a year and half before our lady met Julian Kingsley, one Partick Samuel Riley, bachelor, was wed to Veeda Eileen *Corcoran,* spinster."

"Aha. So Simon's pal, Mick Corcoran, is no doubt the brother Veeda is trying to protect from the sinister—and blood-dripping—Riley?"

"Yes, Watson. Elementary, as Holmes never actually said."

"It couldn't be another Corcoran, could it? It's not exactly an unusual name."

"But Jane, my love, you *saw* our Mick Corcoran outside Veeda's flat in Kilburn the first time you visited her!"

"So I did."

"Then, on your second visit, Veeda implies she knows some pretty rough customers who might have done Julian in, and lo! enter the estranged husband oozing his life's blood on the stairs."

"Yes. I wonder what had happened to Riley that day?"

"Dishonor among thieves, perhaps? Or a skirmish with the police."

"But if it were the police, wouldn't it have been in the news?"

Not if they want to keep it quiet. If it's part of a larger investigation, and they were lucky enough not to have any newshawks get wind of it, they might well keep it under wraps. Since Riley escaped from their clutches, they may be doubly grateful if the word doesn't get out.''

"I see."

James leaned forward. "And now for the news from MacDougal.''

"That dear man! What has he come up with?''

"Two things. First, he found another chap who drives for City Freight Services and learned that Corcoran's firm has a rapid turnover of its staff. This driver had been with them three months and had just been given his notice. Evidently, they don't want anyone around long enough to discover what's going on.

"The fellow was mad as a hornet and told Mac-Dougal he was suspicious of the whole operation but had no proof of anything. Twice he had made runs to Liverpool, but not to one of the usual docks. Each time he was not allowed to supervise the unloading of the cargo. He had noticed some of the crates were labelled Machine Parts, but knew nothing further.''

"Does Liverpool mean anything?''

James looked arch. "Only that it's the major point of departure for Ireland!''

"Shades of the IRA?''

"That seems to be the idea.''

"And what is MacDougal's second bit of news?''

"With his prodigious talent for making contacts, he has found a local policeman here in Burling who, over a second pint, confided that the fire in your burning house on the marsh was not caused by a heater but by an impressive cache of explosives. There wasn't much left of the man listed as Oliver Brown, but there was plenty of evidence that he was in the business of making bombs.''

"Lucky for Riccardo the explosion didn't happen five minutes sooner!''

James choked. "Lucky for you, little Jeanne d'Arc, that there wasn't a second one just as you put your helpful little head in the window!"

I laughed. "Anyhow, we seem to be fraught with suggestions about the Irish Republican Army. But can we find any connection?"

"Do you remember the snatches of conversation you heard between Mick Corcoran and Simon in the lorry?"

I frowned. "Simon referred to someone who was forever going on about the old days and the smuggling. That was how he learned about the underground cache."

"Yes. And what about having lost one hiding place and that was why they needed another?"

"Of course! They were desolate when they lost 'poor old Ollie's place'!"

"Precisely."

I mused. "That's all very well, but how can we prove any connection? Simon and Corcoran are certainly not going to admit to knowing the man Brown, if indeed they did know him."

"Never fear—MacDougal to the rescue! He remembered the mention of 'poor old Ollie' and had one of his investigators ring up Simon and say he was Ollie's brother, and would it be safe to claim the body? You see, the police have noted the suspicious fact that no one has come forward to claim what remains of Brown, if that is his name."

"What did Simon say?"

"Aha! Simon said, *I didn't know Ollie had a brother!*"

"Well, done, MacDougal! Then what?"

"Then, Simon stammered a bit and said, 'I'll get on to Mick and ring you back.' "

"Of course, our man said, 'No, I'll get back to you,' and rang off."

Now I looked at James and the glee subsided from both our faces.

"What do we do now?" James asked gloomily.

"Yes, I see the dilemma. If we go to the police with what we know, Simon will be in it up to his neck. There's no way to protect Bettina from finding out what he's been up to."

"There's another factor, Jane. The police will want to know what first put us onto the information and that means revealing your little jaunt in the back of the lorry. These people are not your garden-variety criminals, they are terrorists, and they can play very rough."

I mused. "On the other hand, darling, they may blow up innocent people any day in the week, and we can scarcely sit by and let that happen."

"Perhaps the best thing is to give an anonymous tip to the police. MacDougal and friends can take care of that."

"Of course. Shall we ring him now?"

"Not on the local telephone exchange. When we're back in London tomorrow, we can ring him from the flat."

"Yes, good idea." I sighed and slipped down against the pillows.

Now James's clear blue eyes filled with concern. "How's the head feeling?"

"Much better, darling." I glanced at the clock. "Time for you to meet Andrew. Will you ask them to send up a sandwich and a glass of milk, please?"

An hour later, when the doctor made his return visit, he confirmed that there was no serious injury. The lassitude I felt was to be expected, and except for a painful knob on the back of my head, I would be fit to resume normal activity by evening.

Moments later, Bettina arrived.

"Jane, darling, are you really all right?"

"Yes, absolutely. The doctor was here and I'm perfectly fit. Just malingering!"

We had given out the story that I fell on the stairs at the Dolphin and struck my head on a newel post, a tale made plausible by the picturesque but torturous passages and uneven flooring of the ancient inn.

"So, Bettina, about Simon—?"

"Yes. For the past six months, since he began working with City Freight Services, he has had rather irregular hours with the firm. Sometimes they seem to have great flurries of activity and at others, the orders fall off and he has a good deal of free time. I'm sure many business enterprises fluctuate in that way, don't they?"

"I should think so."

"The thing is, Jane, in the past two months or so he has been in and out at odd hours of the night, whereas in the past his duties were more often during daytime hours."

"How did he happen to take the job in the first place?"

"Mr. Corcoran is the manager of the company, and when he needed an assistant, he approached Simon."

"Where did Simon meet Corcoran?"

"Actually, I'm not sure. I expect someone introduced them."

"But did Simon have any experience in the field?"

"No, not really." Bettina flushed slightly. "Mr. Corcoran wanted someone to invest in the firm and then learn the workings from the inside, as it were. Simon was quite keen, and I thought it would be a good thing for him to have an enterprise in which he

152

had a vested interest, so to speak. I have a bit of money of my own, so I put in two thousand pounds."

"I see. What does Simon say about the night hours?"

"Oh, he pretends it's a nuisance, but I think he really doesn't mind. What worries me, Jane, is that Simon seems to have changed in some way I can't quite define."

"Is he worried or upset?"

"No, quite the contrary. It's as if he's rather excited about something but can't tell me what it is."

I took a deep breath. "Bettina, darling, I know this is a rotten thing to say, but is it possible—that is—"

Bettina giggled. "Oh, Jane, I know what you're thinking, but I'm sure he doesn't have a lady-friend."

Reluctant to dampen such touching confidence, I said cautiously, "They say the wife is the last to know."

Now her enormous eyes glowed. "But he's very attentive, Jane. Last night, for example, he went down to sleep in the study—he often does that so as not to disturb me when he's out at night—but you see, he didn't leave right away. When we got back from the party onstage—" Blushing like a schoolgirl, she half whispered, "He came to bed, and then dressed and slipped away. He's always so thoughtful."

"You're probably quite right. I know Simon adores you. He's told me so." I didn't add that Simon's last declaration to that effect was in this very room after he tried to make love to me.

"No," Bettina went on, "that's not what troubles me. It's Mr. Corcoran. I almost never see him, and when I do, he avoids my eye and skims off as quickly as he can. There's something odd about him, Jane. I have a dreadful feeling he may be drawing Simon into some kind of trouble."

153

Oh, dear. Was this the time to tell all? No, better wait. After all, what could Bettina do about it at this point, even if she was told all our suspicions? Unhappily, she would know soon enough.

I temporized by promising to keep alert to anything that might be learned about Mick Corcoran, and we went on to other topics.

"Your friend Andrew is so charming, Jane. How's your book coming?"

I laughed. "That's a dangerous question, Bettina. It's like the old saying among graduate students: never ask candidates about their dissertations because they're likely to go on for hours."

I did in fact chat on for a bit about the project until a tap on the door produced Riccardo, dark eyes woeful.

Kissing first me, then Bettina, then me again, Riccardo exclaimed, "Ah, my lovely Jane. I just learned about your fall! You are all right? Let me see!"

Gently feeling the lump on my head, he clucked. "These stairways, so steep, so crooked. I almost fall each day. Yet the inn is so lovely, yes?"

Laughing and talking, we heard another tap at the door.

Looking at her watch, Bettina started for the door. "That may be Simon. He's to call for me."

I wasn't sure I was ready to see Simon. My head had begun to ache, and the sight of Simon's smiling face did nothing to ease the pain.

His kiss was brotherly as he bent over me. "Feeling better?"

"Yes, much," I lied.

On our subsequent meetings after the evening he had come here to my room, Simon had behaved precisely as if nothing had happened. I supposed that in fact, from his point of view, nothing *had* happened.

Making a pass at his wife's friend would be all in the day's—or night's—work to Simon.

As the four of us talked about the success of this year's festival at Southmere, Riccardo, not sharing the English constraint against emotional topics, squeezed Bettina's hand. "It is so sad your dear uncle did not live to enjoy."

Instant tears filling her great eyes, Bettina put out her hand to Riccardo, saying simply, "Thank you." Then she turned to Simon, who put his arm around her and kissed the top of her head.

Now James came in, and there was a general shuffling about as the visitors took their leave. Riccardo went out first. Then, as Simon held the door for Bettina, I happened to glance down at his feet.

He was wearing white running shoes, somewhat the worse for wear, and on the side of the shoe facing me, someone had marked a thick black X.

19

By the time I set off with James and Andrew for that evening's performance of *The Turn of the Screw*, my head was considerably better and the twinges from my assorted bruises were subsiding.

Since the opera is not often performed, this was Andrew's first opportunity to see Benjamin Britten's small masterpiece, and he was not disappointed. On this, their third and final performance of the Southmere season, the singers gave their all, deftly supported by Russell Ames's ensemble in the pit.

Afterward, champagne flowed at the lavish cast party which Julian had established as a Southmere tradition in the first two years of the festival. Our plates heaped with lobster salad and caviar, we stood about smiling as the two children in the cast were allowed small glasses of champagne.

There was no sign of Margot, who had evidently used up her small stock of sociability the evening before. Simon oozed charm on the soprano who sang the role of the governess while Russell stood at Bettina's side repressing a lean and hungry look. Andrew also gazed at her with frank admiration.

None of the *Traviata* cast was present, even those who had remained in Burling. Riccardo was no doubt off with his lady, having recovered his strength after his performance the preceding evening.

As the party at last began to disperse, James and I saw Andrew standing alone, staring up at the empty box where Margot and Julian had sat on the night of the murder. I was about to say "Ready, Andrew?" when we heard an ethereal sound—a phrase of music from the closing scene of the opera—and realized it was Andrew whistling, and quite unaware of his own action.

I smiled at James as we both waited for Andrew to emerge from his trance. It was not the first time I had seen Andrew do this, and on each occasion it had signalled a moment of illumination, a kind of Joycean epiphany.

Back at the Dolphin, the three of us decided on a nightcap and headed for the bar, joined by Raymond Flynt, who came to the foot of the staircase as we passed.

Joyfully beaming, he announced, more like a father than a husband, "Time Ilena came to bed."

As we went down a passage and turned toward the bar, we stopped abruptly. In a dark corner under the stairs, Dmitri Mikos was holding Ilena in his arms, kissing her so passionately that she bent backward in his embrace. Then she began to struggle, crying out, "No, Dmitri, no!"

Raymond pushed past us, taking two strides toward the pair. His voice mild but surprisingly authoritative, he said, "All right, Dmitri."

Dmitri scowled angrily but nevertheless went quickly past us and out through the entrance door to the inn.

Without another word, Raymond took Ilena's arm and guided her past us and up the stairs, and for the first time since I had known him, Raymond was not smiling.

The next morning, we set off after an early breakfast to drive Andrew to Heathrow, where he would catch his plane for Los Angeles. James and I would then go back to town, where I would stay over and return to Southmere on Monday.

The day was cold but beautifully clear, Thursday night's storm seeming to have blown away October's gray canopy.

As James drove, I turned to face Andrew in the back. "Why would Simon mark large X's on his sneakers? James thinks they might have been relics of his university days."

James laughed. "What undergraduates do rarely derives from logic."

Andrew nodded. "Exactly. There's another possibility. Does he belong to some sort of athletic club?"

"Yes, I'm sure I've heard Bettina speak of Simon going to his workout. Their flat in London is in Kensington. The club is probably nearby."

"Then he might have marked them to avoid confusion in the locker room."

"Yes. But if Simon really was one of the two men who robbed Wilkins's gunsmith shop that night, wouldn't he have been careful not to wear shoes that could be identified?"

Andrew said, "He may be so accustomed to seeing them he forgets they are marked. And the robbery took place in the dark. It probably never occurred to him—if it *was* Simon—that anyone would see his shoes. It took a twelve-year-old boy to spot them!"

James added, "More than that, such an identification would never hold up in court. There could be dozens of men all over the British Isles who mark X's on their shoes."

I remembered the evening when Simon had come to my room and I suspected in the end that he was pumping me about James's case. Having given an edited version of Simon's visit, I said now, "It's ironic that Simon might actually have learned something useful if I had chattered freely about the Dan Hawks case to him. When he first queried me, I didn't know about Tommy Wilkins and the shoes, but if I had mentioned it to him later on, he would certainly have lost no time disposing of those shoes."

"Of course it's all speculation on our part," Andrew put in. "Simon may have had no idea that Wilkins's shop even exists."

"Oh, but he did! One day not long before I went down to Southmere, Bettina and Simon came by for tea, and afterward we walked along to the greengrocer together, as Bettina needed some items to take home. As we came out with our shopping bags, we found Simon emerging from the gunsmith shop next door. He kept looking back at the shop window as we left, until Bettina teased him about wanting to buy firearms."

"Then Simon may have suggested this particular shop to Corcoran," said James. "It all ties in with the larger picture. If we are in fact dealing with people who are smuggling supplies to the IRA, what they want are explosives and firearms, especially rifles and handguns, as I understand it. If we can tie the break-in at Wilkins's shop with the operation in Sussex, we may have something useful."

Andrew mused. "If I remember correctly, one of the men was described as taller than the other. Now, if Simon and his pal Mick Corcoran were in this together, do they fit that description?''

James looked at me. ''What do you think, Jane? We saw Corcoran briefly on the night of Julian's murder. I'd have said medium height, wouldn't you? And we know Simon is tall—probably close to six feet.''

"Yes. And when I was in the back of the lorry, I remember that when I looked up, above the space where I was hiding, I could see all of Simon's head over the backboard but only the top of Corcoran's red hair!''

"If only we had a shred of proof.''

Then Andrew said, ''What about the ski mask? Have the police checked it for hair?''

"Oh, good point!'' James smiled. ''They may have done so already, and not finding evidence of hair from either Dan Hawks or his cohort, they've said nothing about it. I'll check that with them first thing tomorrow.''

"But James,'' I objected, ''if the police had found hair belonging to another person, and not to their suspect, and not revealed it, wouldn't that be withholding evidence?''

"Not precisely. They may certainly say that the mask could have been borrowed or stolen, and worn only on the one occasion by one of our chaps—not long enough to leave his hair as a calling card.''

"I see. But if they found hair from either Simon or Corcoran, that's a different story.''

"Exactly.''

As we approached the airport at Heathrow, watching for the signs to Terminal 3, a large lorry passed us just before a turn-off junction, momentarily obliterating the signpost. Just as James slowed, unsure of his direction, the lorry passed on and the crucial sign leapt into view in time for him to make the correct turn.

Suddenly, Andrew gave what could only be described as a yelp. "That's it! Something's been nagging at the edge of my mind since last evening, and I think I've got it! Wait till you've parked the car, and I'll see what you think of it."

When James had found a spot on the third level of the car park and switched off the motor, we both turned to Andrew, who began rather diffidently.

"I've been haunted by things that appear and disappear. It all started last night at the opera, with the illusion of the ghosts of Quint and Miss Jessel. Then, moments ago, the signpost for Terminal 3 was clearly visible, abruptly obscured, and back in view."

"Yes?" I prompted.

"Well, it occurred to me that we may have been subjected to a similar illusion on the night of the murder. What if Julian Kingsley wasn't actually there in the box with Margot when she raised her voice for everyone to hear and told him to go?"

"But I saw them myself. They were both in the box when I was sitting in the stalls."

"Yes, but you went backstage about twenty minutes before seven, Jane. From where you stood in the wings, could you actually *see* Julian?"

"No, you're right. He was behind the curtain."

"Could anyone on the stage or in the orchestra see him?"

"No, not really. Since Margot was speaking to him, we naturally assumed he was there."

"Yes. But what if Julian had already gone and she was speaking to an empty chair?"

James mused. "You're saying Julian may have left sometime earlier than we were told. In that case, wouldn't someone have seen him as he left the box?"

161

"No, evidently not. Yesterday, when Jane showed me around the theater, we went into the Kingsley box, and I particularly remember that the door into the corridor was directly behind Julian's chair, at the far end of the box, not in the center, as one might expect."

"Yes, I see. If no one saw him leave at shortly before seven, by the same token he could have slipped out earlier and not have been seen."

"Exactly. To reach the tower, he would no doubt have gone out on the house side of the theater and taken the path up the hill from there."

After a moment of silence, I said, "Wait! Someone actually heard Julian answer Margot when she told him to go. Who was it? Oh, I remember. It was Anton Szabo. He was standing more or less under the Kingsley box, and he told Sergeant Glenn he thought he heard Julian mutter something but he couldn't catch the words."

James said, "Yes, but don't we often hear what we expect to hear? I've had witnesses in court who were positive they heard sounds of all sorts because it was logical that such sounds were present."

Andrew added, "Or, Margot may well have made such a sound herself. She might have cried out, 'Go on then, I don't give a damn,' and then made a low gurgling sound which would pass for an answer in case anyone could hear!"

We were all silent again, sharing the thought that Andrew at last expressed. "Obviously, if all this isn't a mad pipe dream on my part, it means that Julian could have been killed at least ten minutes *before* seven o'clock, and that Margot was providing an alibi for someone. A hired killer? Her mysterious lover? Who knows?"

James said, "That could open up some interesting

possibilities. We can still rule out the orchestra and chorus, the stage crew and front staff, all of whom were accounted for straight through from the beginning of the dress rehearsal. There were others for whom the ten minutes would make no difference, I suppose."

"Yes," Andrew nodded. "Simon was dressing at the house; Dr. Raymond was in his box, watching the rehearsal; Riccardo was in his dressing room, with no witnesses. What about Dmitri Mikos?"

I said, "Technically, it's possible. He's not onstage at that time, and comes back for his offstage part of the duet, but there's a problem. If a singer left the theater and went out into the cold, even for ten minutes, his voice would undoubtedly be affected, and I must say he sounded fine to me from where I stood in the wings."

James said, "Specifically, we are looking for someone who has the classic ironclad alibi for seven o'clock but none for ten minutes before seven."

Triumphantly, I cried, "Yes! Someone who walked into a pub in Burling at seven o'clock, started playing darts and eating shepherd's pie, but who might have been anywhere before that. *Mick Corcoran!*"

20

Half an hour later, Andrew had gone through to the departure lounge at Terminal 3 for his 12:30 flight, while James and I had decided it was time for lunch and adjourned to the cafeteria-style coffee shop. Sundays were busy days at airports everywhere, and Heathrow was no exception. By the time we had queued up and slowly made our way along to the end of the line, even the bland food on my tray began to look edible.

Squeezing into a narrow plastic booth, we sorted out our plates and teacups, and between bites, went over again the possibilities uncovered by Andrew's inspired theory about Margot and the empty box.

We agreed that previously the problem had been to find any sort of motive for those who had the opportunity to murder Julian. Unless the killer was a stranger, hired by Margot, or on the other hand, a member of the IRA group who wanted to dispose of Julian for their own purposes, the short list of available suspects from members of the Southmere Festival offered little scope.

James swallowed a bite of sandwich. "Once Mick

Corcoran becomes a possibility, it all makes sense. Margot insisted that Julian was planning to meet someone at seven o'clock, but we have only her word for that. In fact, the appointment was probaby for a quarter of seven or thereabouts all along.

"Corcoran is waiting at the tower for Julian, knocks him on the head, pitches him over the balcony, and bob's-your-uncle! He nips into Burling and strolls into the pub, casual as you please, greeting acquaintances, perhaps even calling attention to the time without anyone being the wiser. Then he comes back to the tower at shortly before nine o'clock, establishing the story that his appointment with Julian was at that time all along."

I nodded. "Now there are two possibilities. Was Corcoran hired by Margot, in which case his motive nicely coincides with the interests of his terrorist connections? Or, *is Mick Corcoran Margot's lover?*"

James smiled. "I rather fancy him as the mystery lover. If he's merely a hit man, why the elaborate setting up of an alibi? He could take a potshot at Julian any time. But if the master plan is to establish a dawning love, leading eventually to marriage, it would be vital to have the lucky man in the clear!"

I felt a surge of joy, not merely because we had found the solution to the murder of Julian Kingsley, but because James could speak with such casual amusement of Margot and her affairs. Whatever vestiges of pity or concern may have lingered toward his former love had clearly vanished, and as the Bard would have it, left not a rack behind.

Now James went on. "So what do we do about this, my sweet? It's ever so ingenious, and it makes eminently good sense to us, but selling this to Detective

Chief Inspector Collier, who's in charge of the Kingsley murder case, is another kettle of fish.

"The IRA connection should be clear sailing for the police. Once they know of the underground cache and the activities of City Freight Services, Ltd., as well as the tie-in with Oliver Brown and the exploding house on the marsh, they should be able to round up the whole gang and have them in custody in due course. I'm afraid Simon will simply have to take his lumps along with his chum Corcoran. But where does that leave us with the murder of Kingsley?"

"Yes, darling, I see the problem. The inspector will simply give us that skeptical eyebrow he favored us with on the night he came to the flat. I can hear him now: 'A clever ploy to get yourself in the clear, my dear chap, but have you an ounce of proof?' "

"Exactly. So what proof can we find?"

"Well, we could begin with Mrs. Lacey at the antique shop. If she identifies Mick Corcoran as 'Mr. Smith,' it will be a big nail in his coffin. I'll try her first thing tomorrow."

As James was about to reply, we felt the floor of the terminal building shake beneath us. The table between us careened into the air, scattering its contents, and at the same moment we heard the ear-splitting roar of an explosion in the open area of the terminal, perhaps thirty yards away.

Then began the screams of the terrified and the wounded, and the chaos of people running. Stunned, I looked at James and saw blood pouring from his forehead. Snatching a couple of paper tissues from my handbag, I wiped at the blood and saw what appeared to be a two-inch cut, not as deep as I had feared.

"Hold this, darling. Press hard!"

"Yes, all right. It's nothing, really."

Slowly, we made our way toward the scene of devastation, where security guards and police were already converging, and the *squee-squaa* of ambulances were soon heard outside on the lower level.

There was little doubt that a bomb had been detonated. The mangled bodies of two men lay on the carpeted area, among shattered bits of metal and upholstery that had once been seats for waiting passengers. A small boy, screaming "Mummy! Mummy!" was held back by a blood-splashed man who stared in anguish at the young woman on the floor at his feet, to whom a man, obviously a doctor, was administering aid.

Some of the wounded screamed piteously, while others lay silently gazing at the helpless spectators. All of this we saw in brief glimpses, before a throng of medics arrived to take the injured to hospitals.

Now came hours of police questioning before anyone was permitted to leave. Andrew's flight had long since gone, but all flights after the bombing were cancelled until released by the authorities.

It was late afternoon before we reached our flat, exhausted but incredibly grateful that we were safe. The cut on James's forehead, evidently caused by flying crockery, had proved to be as superficial as I had hoped.

From the television, we learned that four people had died and a dozen others were injured, some critically. A splinter group of the IRA had claimed responsibility for the bombing.

Grimly, James reached for the telephone. "This can't wait for tomorrow, Jane. I'm ringing MacDougal now."

Within the hour, MacDougal arrived at the flat, shaking his head at our narrow escape from annihilation at the airport.

Then, bent double over his knees, notebook in hand,

he looked up at James. "Time to get after these buggers, eh? Begging your pardon, Mrs. H."

Carefully, we reviewed all the information we had gathered on the case, outlining Andrew's theory about Margot and the empty box.

MacDougal looked down at his notes. "I'll run down to Burling now. After today's bombing, the police will be getting hundreds of telephone tips. This is best done in person."

James said, "Of course you needn't give the sources for your information."

"Righto. No need to mention Mrs. H. at all. They'll be glad enough to get any leads to IRA activity, whether this group or another did the job today. As for the Kingsley murder, while our chap Corcoran is under suspicion for robbery and smuggling, we'll have time to get the evidence we need. Suppose he's taken into custody and our lady is foolish enough to stand bail for him or otherwise tip her hand? It would give us something to go on."

When MacDougal had gone, we sank into exhausted silence, glumly watching the news on the television as it went over and over the events of the bombing at Heathrow.

The ring of the telephone seemed like an intrusion from another world. I heard James say, "Yes, she's here," and reluctantly I took the receiver from him.

What I heard brought me to instant alertness: a harsh, gravelly voice, almost a whisper. "Jane? Veeda Riley here. Can you come?"

"Yes, Veeda, of course. I'll be there straight away!"

"James! This is it! Veeda may be fond of her brother, but if she found out he killed Julian—"

James reached for his coat. "You're not going alone, Jane. These people are dangerous. If she won't talk in my presence, I'll wait outside."

168

While London traffic was never light, Sunday evenings were far better than weekdays, and we made it to Kilburn in less than half an hour. Parking on Veeda's street was another matter, but James managed to squeeze into a spot half a dozen houses away, and we hurried back and up the stairs to the top flat of 20 Gorston Road.

No one answered my knock.

"Veeda!" I called, softly at first, then loudly.

Nothing.

James reached for the doorknob without the least hope. No one in London failed to lock their doors, night or day.

When the door slowly opened at his touch, we gaped in surprise, and took a few tentative steps into the room. There was the gold plush sofa where I had sat on two occasions, with Veeda's deep chair opposite and the marble-topped coffee table between, with its familiar bottle of sherry and the arrangement of artificial flowers.

"Veeda!" I called again. Together, we walked through the dining ell into the kitchen, seeing no one.

A few steps down the passage was the bedroom, and there, on the floor, lay Veeda Riley, facing us on her side, her reddish hair spread out on the carpet.

While James sprang for the phone to dial 999, I fell to my knees beside Veeda and grasped her arm. It was warm to the touch, and now I could hear her shallow, labored breathing.

"She's alive," I called to James, who gave the address, urging speed to the emergency operator.

When I stood up, I saw what hadn't been apparent at first in the darkened bedroom. The knees of my jeans were red with blood, from a pool which had formed in front of Veeda's chest.

I snatched the down comforter from the bed and

covered her, feeling utterly helpless to do anything further until help arrived. Kneeling again and holding her hand, I murmured, "It's all right, Veeda. The ambulance is coming." Over and over, I repeated my phrases of reassurance, having no idea whether or not she could hear me.

When at last she was borne away, I picked up her handbag from the dressing table and found the keys to the flat. Locking the door after us, we took her handbag with us and drove to the hospital where the attendants had told us she would be taken.

After half an hour in the emergency waiting room, while a child with a cut hand was treated and a woman moaning with abdominal pain was left waiting for what I thought was an inordinate length of time, we were suddenly confronted with a detective sergeant and a constable. They regarded us with deep suspicion.

When we had identified ourselves and handed over Veeda's handbag, the sergeant led us into an empty room along the passage. With the constable standing by, the sergeant turned to James. "You have the right to remain silent," he began, in the familiar caution against self-incrimination. Ignoring James's protest, he finished the ritual, then gave me the same recitation.

James said mildly, "We have nothing to conceal, Sergeant. How can we help you?"

Somewhat mollified, the sergeant explained what we had already suspected. "The victim suffered a gunshot wound in the chest. Our men will be searching her flat now. Did you see a weapon at the scene or have you any knowledge of such a weapon?"

That was only the beginning. We answered repeated questions about our acquaintance with Veeda Riley, which I explained as clearly as I could, beginning with my work at the Southmere Festival and the hope that

Mrs. Riley might have some knowledge that would relate to the murder of Julian Kingsley.

I recounted my two visits with her, neither of which produced any helpful information, except for her promise to tell me if she ever learned that anyone known to her had been involved in the death of Julian.

"And when she rang you up today, what did she say?"

"She asked if I would come to see her, and I said I would be there as quickly as I could."

"Do you believe she now had the information she had referred to before?"

"I certainly hoped that was why she wanted to speak to me, but as you see, she was unconscious when we arrived."

James said, "This crime was not a break-in, Sergeant. The door to the flat was unlocked when we arrived, and nothing appeared to be disturbed. I trust you will keep a guard on Mrs. Riley's room. Whoever tried to kill her may come back, and it could very well be a family member!"

"And who might that be, sir?"

"This is conjecture only, you understand, but I should keep an eye out for her estranged husband, Patrick Riley, and a chap named Mick Corcoran, who we believe is her brother."

When the sergeant learned that one or both of these men might not only be a murder suspect but might also have a connection with the IRA, although we had no proof of this, he was jolted into action. After the appalling tragedy at Heathrow that afternoon, any police officer who produced a lead in that case would be heaped with laurels.

Over and over we answered the same questions,

until at last the sergeant told us we might go, warning James that he should remain available for further questioning.

"That's an understatement," James said to me wryly. "I'll probably have half of Scotland Yard on the doorstep tomorrow!"

21

Back in Burling the next morning, I went straight to the antique shop to ask Mrs. Lacey to describe Margot's mysterious Mr. Smith, and found her assistant there instead.

"Mrs. Lacey won't be in today. She buys on Mondays, you see."

Swallowing my chagrin, I wrote the phone number of the Dolphin on my card and asked that she ring me as soon as possible on an urgent matter.

At Southmere, I found a distraught Bettina, sitting at her desk but unable to concentrate.

"Jane, thank heaven you're here! The police have taken Simon in for questioning. It's nothing to do with Uncle Julian—at least, I don't believe so. It's all to do with Mr. Corcoran and City Freight Services. You see, just as I feared—Simon must have been drawn into some sort of trouble!"

Heart-stricken at the disillusionment in store for Bettina, I shifted to the topic of the bombing at Heathrow the afternoon before, describing the horror of the scene and our fortuitous escape.

"Oh, Jane! Thank God you were safe. And Andrew?"

"His flight had gone while we were eating our lunch."

Now the tasks of the day bore in upon us. With tonight's performance of *Traviata*, the festival came to an end, and Bettina was busy with details. I had agreed to stay on until Wednesday to help with the final wrap-up.

Without taking a lunch break, we had sandwiches sent over from the house and worked through until teatime.

"That's it, Jane!" Bettina tidied her desk, then sat toying with the two jade monkeys left in their box. "Whatever could have happened to little Speak No Evil? One of the cleaners must have knocked it off into the wastepaper basket without realizing it."

Reaching for my coat, I muttered agreement, feeling guilt-stricken at the number of things I could not divulge to my friend.

Now those lovely eyes filled with tears. "Four o'clock and no word from Simon. It must be something dreadful, Jane."

Driving back to the Dolphin, I wondered how Veeda Riley was progressing. We had rung up the hospital in the morning and, after much reluctance, were told that the surgery had been successful and she was "resting comfortably," the classic euphemism for "at least she's alive." Yes, her room was guarded and no visitors were allowed. How long would it be, I wondered, before I would learn what she wanted to tell me?

Our phone had been busy in the hour before I left London. Andrew had called from Los Angeles, horrified when he saw the television coverage of the Heathrow bombing and grateful to learn that we were safe.

He had also added something that puzzled me at the time.

"Jane, I've been thinking about when you were being lured up the stairs of the tower and your assailant, pretending to be Bettina, called out 'Hurry up!' You felt there was something wrong but you didn't know what it was."

"Yes, I remember."

"It seems to me that phrase is typically American. Bettina might say 'Come quickly!' or even 'Hurry!' but she probably wouldn't say 'Hurry *up!*' This may be what sounded wrong to you."

"Yes," I had agreed. "I think you're right.'

Afterwards, James had said, "A good many Brits pick up Americanisms. We don't know enough about Mick Corcoran's speech to judge whether this applies to him, but it seems likely enough."

After Andrew's call, James had rung up the local detective who was in charge of the Dan Hawks case and asked for a report on hair samples in the ski mask found on the pavement just beyond Wilkins's shop. After some shuffling of papers, he was told that such a report had been made and considered irrelevant, since the only hairs found were carroty red, while both suspects were brown haired!

Hastily, James reported the whole story of Mick Corcoran and Simon Barnes, setting the wheels in motion for a new slant on the case.

As I was leaving, James was asked to meet with detectives at New Scotland Yard, as he had expected, to tell what he could about potential IRA connections.

At last, I reached the Dolphin and was heading for my room and the prospect of a bath, when Raymond Flynt called out from the residents' lounge, "Jane, come and have tea with me!"

Why not, I thought. There was plenty of time before dressing.

Fixed grin in place, Raymond made room for me on a tapestry sofa and ordered another pot.

"I see you've been converted to the British afternoon ritual, Raymond."

"Yes. When in Rome, you know."

"How's Ilena?"

"She's resting before tonight's performance. You know, Jane, I didn't know a thing about singers till I married one. It's quite a production. They need all sorts of coddling. And of course, Ilena's especially insecure."

My tea arrived and I gratefully poured out a steaming cup. The English belief that most things can be set right by a nice cup of tea is not far wrong.

Beaming, Raymond went on. "Ilena's family were political refugees from Argentina, you know. Fortunately, they brought plenty of money with them. When she came to the States as a teenager, she studied voice with the best coaches in Los Angeles, won a major competition. Everything was coming up roses, but still she had problems of self-image and identification. That's how she came to me."

"She was your patient, Raymond?"

"Oh, yes, all my wives were my patients!"

Startled, I longed to ask how many there had been but delicacy held me back. I needn't have worried. Life to Raymond knew no reticence.

"Yes, Ilena's my third wife. Funny, isn't it? I'm still on friendly terms with the first two. I don't know what they see in me, but that's the way it is!"

I wondered, too. Raymond certainly wasn't my cup of tea, but there's no accounting for tastes.

Needing no prompting, Raymond went on. "You probably wondered about that little incident last night with Ilena and Dmitri? Well, she needs lots of admiration, especially from men, to bolster her self-confidence, so I like to give her plenty of space."

Too much space? I wondered.

"But she doesn't actually want things to go too far, so I'm sort of standing by to protect her, if you see what I mean?"

"Yes, of course."

When I finally reached my room and sank into a hot bath, I reflected on the infinite variety of relationships within that elastic condition called marriage. If Raymond and Ilena had found an arrangement that worked for them, who was I to see anything odd about it?

Before leaving for the theater, I had a call from Bettina. She was going to wait at the police station until they gave her news of Simon, and would I please look after things and do the honors for her at the cast party? Whatever happened, she was utterly unable to make an appearance.

"But Jane, do come to the house afterward, please!"

I promised, offering what condolences I could muster.

Fortunately, there were no problems at the theater. The final performance was inspired, and afterward everyone was euphoric. The caterers supplied the same delicious buffet we had had on Saturday evening, but this time to a much larger group. The stage crew and front staff, the musicians from orchestra and chorus, the singers and the conductor—everyone slurped champagne and toasted the success of the festival.

It was midnight before Russell Ames and I bid the last participant good night and closed the theater.

"You've been marvelous, Russell," I said, giving

him the ritual theatrical kiss on the cheek. "Are you leaving tomorrow?"

"Yes, back to London. And you?"

"Not until Wednesday."

Then, believing that she was ill, he asked, "Is there anything I can do for Bettina?"

"No, thank you, Russell dear."

He would know the truth soon enough. I wondered if someday in the future he might be around to pick up the pieces if Bettina's world fell apart.

22

At the main house of Southmere, I went to the family entrance off the pantry, where old Alfred opened the door for me.

"Good evening, Miss Jane. Miss Bettina will see you in the small study."

As Alfred took my coat, he said, "Mrs. Kingsley is in the morning room with Mr. Szabo. She will join you later."

Anton here? Probably making his pitch for Margot to continue the festival next year, with him as Grand Mogul. I wondered if he'd have any luck. Julian's will had provided some funds for continuing the festival, but it would take more than that to keep it going.

But why would Margot join us later? Bettina would have told her about Simon's arrest by now. Will she offer help? Perhaps pay for a solicitor for Simon? Oh, no, I thought, not James, if that's what she has in mind. Emphatically no.

As I passed the door of the morning room, I heard Margot's voice sounding rather shrill, and low murmurs from Anton. Good luck to the Hungarian genius.

In the small study, I found Bettina sitting before the

fire, her ashen face smudged with dried tears. Taking her hand, I said simply, "Tell me."

"Yes. It's very bad, Jane. Simon has been part of a group that smuggles firearms to Ireland for the IRA."

"Do the police have any proof?"

"Yes, I'm afraid so. He and Mr. Corcoran were caught this morning as they loaded some crates onto a boat at Burling Harbor."

"Oh, I see. Simon is being held in custody?"

"Yes."

"Then how did you learn about it?"

"About ten o'clock this evening, they finally let me see Simon for a few minutes. He has admitted everything to the police."

"What did he tell you?"

"It all started, of course, with that man Corcoran. When Simon first joined the firm, he had no idea there was anything illegal about it. He noticed that Corcoran handled all the business end and didn't give Simon much chance to deal with orders, and so on, but you know Simon. He isn't terribly keen on being an executive type. He rather liked making runs in the lorries, and sitting about in pubs with the drivers. He'd never encountered that kind of life before, and Simon is quite democratic, you know."

It sounded to me like the eternal small boy playing with a new toy, and in a moment I saw I wasn't far wrong.

"Corcoran told Simon a good many stories about the Irish and how much they hated being ruled by Britain. Corcoran himself was born in London, but his father had been active in 'the troubles' in Northern Ireland, and Mick was raised to believe in the cause. Even so, it was only about two years ago that he became actively involve.

"Years ago, his sister had married a man named

Patrick Riley, who was what Mick called a 'hard-core' activist, and when Mick went into the business, Riley had persuaded Mick to use the freight line for transporting materials. The odd thing, Jane, is that Mick's sister is the Veeda Riley who was Uncle Julian's—er—friend, the one who was mentioned in his will."

"Yes, Bettina, I suspected that. You see, when James was under suspicion for your uncle's murder, I went to see Veeda Riley, hoping she might know something that would give us a clue, but she didn't. Then James learned that Veeda's maiden name was Corcoran, and we thought there might be a connection."

It was as well to tell this now, as I knew that a good deal of the story would come out in the end. The one thing I never wanted Bettina—nor the police—to know about was my journey in the back of the lorry with Simon and Corcoran. After all, I had no idea that day that there was any connection with terrorism, and when MacDougal checked the underground cache, it was empty.

"But go on about Simon," I added.

"It seems that gradually Simon became very keen on the Irish question. I remember now that he has talked a good deal about his sympathy with the cause, but it never occurred to me that it was anything but his usual enthusiasm. When I protested that killing innocent people was wrong, no matter what the ideology behind it, he would sort of agree and then change the subject.

"Now he tells me it all seemed like a game to him. It was frightfully exciting to feel they were evading the customs officers, like the eighteenth-century smugglers that we see in the films. One day, he heard old Alfred talking about the old days and how there was an underground cache right here on the grounds of Southmere.

"But, Jane, it was much more than a game. Simon and Corcoran actually committed a burglary. Very late one night, they broke into a gunsmith shop in your neighborhood in London, and when the proprietor shot at them, Mick returned the fire and the man was wounded. Thank heaven he survived, or they could have been charged with murder!"

"Yes, I know about the crime, Bettina, because James is representing one of the men who was falsely accused."

"That's what Simon told me. They learned all about it soon afterwards."

"Did Simon volunteer this to the police today?"

"No. He was told that the London police were looking for Mick Corcoran because they had found reddish hairs in the ski mask worn by one of the burglars. Since Mick was in custody here, they sent a man down with the evidence, and the hair samples matched. That was when Simon admitted what they had done.

"He was furious with Mick for firing the gun, but what could he do? Simon was beginning to get cold feet about the whole thing, Jane. Do you remember when you saw the house on the marsh that caught fire? It seems the man was one of their group who was making bombs. It was a terrible accident, and Simon was shaken by it. But when he said he was thinking of pulling out, Corcoran just laughed and told him nobody leaves the movement—except feet first.

"Then Simon consoled himself with the belief that it was all for a good cause and they wouldn't be caught anyhow. Now he's terribly remorseful. After the bombing at Heathrow yesterday, it suddenly became real to him, and he realizes what a fool he has been."

"What happened this morning?"

"It seems that yesterday the police here in Sussex received a tip about the underground cache. They put a watch on the place, and early this morning, they saw Simon and Corcoran load some crates onto their lorry and drive to Burling Harbor. Following the lorry, they watched as Simon and Corcoran began to load the cargo onto a boat which would smuggle it across to the Irish coast, and that's when they made the arrest.

"The crates were filled with rifles and handguns! Oh, Jane, how could Simon have been so foolish? My poor darling! He clung to me and wept, and then they took him away."

"Didn't the police tell Simon he could have a solicitor present?"

"Oh, yes, I forgot that part. The only person Simon knew in this part of the world was John Kemp, Uncle Julian's solicitor—the one who drew his will."

"Yes, I remember."

"Mr. Kemp came to the station, but when he heard what the charges were, he was very short with Simon. He told him he himself would not represent him but would recommend someone else. Meanwhile, his advice was to say nothing, to answer no questions.

"At first, Simon tried to follow his advice, but after all, they had been caught in the act, and Simon feels so dreadful about what he's done that he wanted to throw himself on their mercy, so to speak."

James had told me more than once that this is exactly what the inexperienced criminal is likely to do. It's the hardened offenders who shut up like clams under police questioning.

Suddenly, down the passage, we heard the door to the morning room open, and Margot's voice, harsh with fury, cried out, "Come back here at once! You can't mean it—"

Then we heard Anton Szabo's arrogant voice. "Aw, shit, Margot, love's young dream is okay for kids, but come off it—" Then his voice changed to one of pure astonishment. "Hey, put that thing down. Don't be stupid—"

The sound of a gunshot split the air, then two more shots in rapid succession.

In the corridor, we saw the body of Anton Szabo, his head shattered. In the doorway of the morning room, Margot stood staring down at him, a revolver in her hand.

"The bastard!" She spat out the words. "The bloody bastard!"

23

At the sound of the gunshots, old Alfred and other servants of the Southmere household, some in nightwear, came rushing to the scene, staring in horror at the corpse on the floor and at their mistress standing over him, a revolver in her hand. One look at the body of Anton Szabo gave no hope that he could survive.

"I'll ring for the police," said old Alfred simply.

Margot stood for a moment longer, staring down at the body. Then she handed the revolver to Bettina, saying, "It belongs to Simon." Moving like a woman in a trance, she walked slowly into the morning room and sat down, her back to the commotion in the passage. When she spoke, her voice was flat, the anger drained away. "He didn't really love me. He admitted it to me."

Bettina said softly, "Anton was your lover, Margot?"

Margot's eyes turned toward Bettina, then toward me, as if she scarcely recognized us.

"Yes, of course. We kept it from Julian. He told me he would kill me if I left him for another man, so you see, we could never let him know."

Now Margot looked at me. "But Jane, you knew, didn't you? Anton said you must have seen us at the tower. Your car was still in the car park when we left. He waited and saw you drive away."

I held my breath, hoping she would go on, but her voice faded.

"But it doesn't matter now, does it? Nothing matters now."

There was a long silence, while Margot gazed into the fire, utterly oblivious to the sounds behind her.

Then Bettina and I were called into the corridor where we found Sergeant Glenn, the police officer who had questioned everyone at the theater on the night of Julian's murder.

In answer to his question, we told him briefly what had happened. When the ambulance crew arrived, the men looked at the body and shook their heads.

"No hope there, Sergeant."

"No. I've already rung up homicide. The special unit is on its way."

Covering the body of Anton Szabo with a sheet, the ambulance crew stood aside.

Now Sergeant Glenn went into the morning room and spoke to Margot. "You have the right to remain silent," he began.

Suddenly, Margot's eyes were guarded. "Yes?"

Gravely, the sergeant went on. "But anything you do say may be taken down and used in evidence against you."

Now the trancelike state was gone, and the old Margot was back, the eyes cold, the voice arrogant. "Thank you, Sergeant. I have nothing whatever to say."

Half an hour later, Detective Chief Inspector Collier had arrived from police headquarters, while a bevy of technicians swarmed about, taking photographs, fingerprints, measurements—all the paraphernalia of a major crime.

Margot said, "Yes, I shot him," and stuck to her resolution to say no more.

Inspector Collier shrugged and asked Sergeant Glenn to take her to the local police station for the night. "Lady of the manor or not," he growled, "a murder suspect must be held in custody."

In the small study, Collier spoke briefly with Bettina, then asked for me to be sent in.

"Mrs. Hall?" Studying my face, he said, "I believe we've met, have we not?"

"Yes, in London. You were questioning my husband about the murder of Julian Kingsley."

"Of course. And does this present crime bear any relation to that matter?"

I took a deep breath. "Yes, Inspector. It seems quite clear that Anton Szabo, the man Mrs. Kingsley shot, was guilty of murdering Julian Kingsley."

Collier's eyebrow rose in his characteristic gesture. "And how have you reached that conclusion?"

"It's rather a long story—"

His mouth twitched. "I have all the time you like."

"All right, then. You see, unless Julian was killed by someone unknown to us—a hired assassin, for example—we could find no reasonable motive for any of the persons present at the theater that evening who also had the opportunity to leave and return unseen.

"Everyone assumed that the murder took place between seven o'clock and ten minutes or so after seven, when my husband arrived at the car park and found Julian on the walk by the tower. As you are fully aware, the conductor and members of the orchestra were in the pit from half-past six until after seven o'clock, when the first act ended. The chorus were

187

always together, either onstage or in the green room. No members of the stage crew or the front staff was alone and unaccounted for during that time.

"However, several people might have qualified as suspects. Dr. Raymond Flynt, the husband of the soprano, Ilena Santos, claimed to be in a box on the second tier, but no one could confirm his presence there. We had heard a rumor that his wife had carried on a flirtation with Mr. Kingsley some months ago in Salzburg, but it seemed unlikely that this could constitute a motive for murder at this late date.

"The baritone, Riccardo Palma, who does not come on until the second act of the opera, stated that he was in his dressing room warming up, although again no one substantiates his claim. The problem with Riccardo as a suspect is that, not only does he have no motive, he is extremely protective of his voice, and it is impossible to believe he would leave the theater, go out into the cold, commit a murder, and return in time to sing. If he wanted to kill Julian, he would have chosen any time in the world rather than during a dress rehearsal!

"Then there is Simon Barnes, the husband of the lady you spoke with just now. Another rumor suggested that Julian Kingsley, who had disapproved of the match between Simon and his niece, had threatened Simon with exposure for some activity for which Julian was gathering proof. This certainly constituted a more logical motive for Simon, except that so far as we know, Julian had not yet acquired the information he needed. Now, of course, I expect you know that Simon is under arrest for crimes connected with the IRA?"

"My dear young lady, every policeman in the British Isles is acquainted with the arrest of Mr. Barnes and his cohort. I have spent some hours questioning them myself today.''

"I see. Sorry! Well, then, on last Friday evening, the night of the storm, I took shelter on the lower level of the tower at Southmere and inadvertently overheard Margot—Mrs. Kingsley—meeting with someone who was obviously her lover. The affair had been going on for some time, since the burden of Margot's complaint was that when her husband was alive, they had to maintain secrecy, but now that Julian was gone, she wanted to be with her lover openly, not in hidden corners.

"I was not able to identify the man with Margot, and I was certain they had no idea I had overheard them. But later that night, I received a strange message to meet my friend Bettina at the tower. Without a second thought, I dashed off, and at the foot of the winding staircase I heard a voice from above calling me. Naturally, I supposed it was Bettina, and the voice was faint and wavery, sounding as though she was hurt and needed my help.

"Before I reached the top of the stairs, the voice called 'Hurry up!' Something sounded wrong, and I felt vaguely that it was not Bettina calling. Later, when our friend Andrew Quentin suggested that 'Hurry *up*' is more American than British usage, I should have thought then of Anton Szabo, whose speech was decidedly American, but it never entered my mind. I thought only that Mick Corcoran might use that expression.

"Then, at the top of the stairs, someone knocked me on the head and I remember falling.

"When I regained consciousness, I felt something in my hand and later found that it was the figurine of the monkey, Speak No Evil, which I took as a warning. Only I wasn't sure what information I was supposed to possess.''

Collier's eyes stared coolly into mine. "And did you report this incident to the police?''

"No. Actually, I was more frightened than hurt, Inspector, and I felt such a fool. But you see, the episode did reveal one thing which had puzzled us from the beginning. How did anyone persuade Julian Kingsley to go up to the third level of the tower, when they might have conducted their interview on the ground? Now it seemed at least feasible that the same device used for me had been used to lure Julian up the stairs, so that he could be thrown off the balcony of the tower.

"A few minutes ago, before you arrived, Margot told me that Anton saw my car in the car park that night and believed I had seen them together at the tower. Clearly, then, it was Anton who attacked me in the tower, but how could he have murdered Julian when he was present in the theater at the crucial time?

"I believe the answer to that was supplied by Andrew Quentin, after his visit here at Southmere. When Julian watched dress rehearsals and performances, he liked to sit in the corner of his box, looking out through a gap in the curtain, from where he could not be seen from the stage. When we learned that Margot had a lover, and therefore a powerful motive for getting rid of her husband, Andrew posed the question: What if Julian had actually left earlier than we supposed, and Margot had pretended to speak to him in order to provide an alibi for someone who was accounted for at seven o'clock, the presumed time of the murder, but not earlier?

"I confess our favored suspect was none other than Mick Corcoran. He was known to be at a pub in Burling at seven, but not before. We did not consider

Anton Szabo for two reasons. He and Margot appeared to dislike each other intensely. Also, Anton was standing under the Kingsley box and reported that he heard Julian answer Margot when she shouted at him to leave her. Now, of course, it's clear that their mutual hatred was cleverly feigned, and that Anton's evidence about Julian was part of the master plan.

"No one questioned Anton's whereabouts during the rehearsal, because we *knew* where he was at seven o'clock. I saw him at the back of the stalls shortly after the rehearsal began. Then, at a few minutes before seven, he interrupted the rehearsal to give directions to the chorus, obviously a ploy to confirm his presence in the theater. But the period from twenty minutes before seven, when I left to go backstage, until five minutes before seven, when he broke into the rehearsal, are unaccounted for. He simply left the theater *before* Julian, sprinted up to the tower, lured Julian up the stairs, committed the murder, and came back in time to call attention to his presence.

"I believe now that Julian's appointment with Mick Corcoran was indeed for nine o'clock, as Corcoran said it was. Julian no doubt hoped to elicit some information from Corcoran about Simon's activities, maybe even planning to offer him a bribe. In order to change the time of Julian's departure from the theater, it was simple enough for Margot to come over from the main house, join Julian in the box, and tell him a message had come through changing the appointment to a quarter to seven.

"Now that we know Anton Szabo was Margot's lover, it all falls into place. Even from the brief conversation I heard between them that night at the tower, it was evident that Margot was totally obsessed with this man. Tonight, when he rather brutally scoffed at 'love's young dream,' she cracked and killed him."

191

Inspector Collier sat silent for a time. Then the eyebrow went up, but this time there was almost a smile on his lips. "I wouldn't mind having some corroboration. The evidence of you and Mrs. Barnes as to what Mrs. Kingsley said tonight is all very well, but by the time a case gets to court, she'll be denying she ever said a word."

Dejected, I shook my head. "They covered their tracks remarkably well, Inspector."

"I'd especially like some confirmation that this affair was on before the death of the husband."

Then I remembered. "Of course! Mrs. Lacey!"

"Who's Mrs. Lacey?"

"At the antique shop." Reporting the whole incident, I added, "We have dozens of cast photos and rehearsal pictures with Anton and others in a group. I'll get them for you, if you like."

"Right, then. Let's call it a night. I'll be in touch tomorrow."

24

We learned afterward that by noon the next day Detective Chief Inspector Collier had two pieces of evidence that confirmed our theory about the murder of Julian Kingsley.

First, Mrs. Lacey promptly identified Anton Szabo as the young man who had bought Margot's ring. She further remembered that as they were leaving the shop, the man had said, "Wait here, I'll go first," which she thought odd at the time. Now it was clear that the couple did not wish to be seen together.

Second, a crucial piece of evidence came from the lighting assistant at the festival. When the police, that very morning, questioned members of the stage crew and technicians, most of whom were Sussex residents, this man reported that during the first act he was sent to look for Anton Szabo, as his chief wanted to speak to the stage director. At the top of the stairs he saw Anton coming into the theater through a door in the foyer.

"I thought he must have gone out for a smoke," he had said. "Then, the next moment I heard him stop the performance. He was telling the chorus to come back and make their exits again. I went down after that and delivered my message."

When asked why he had not come forward earlier with this information, the technician shrugged. "We were all asked if we had seen Mr. Kingsley. No one asked about Mr. Szabo!"

That morning, I said goodbye to several members of the festival group. Stepping out of the Dolphin for a short walk after breakfast, I met Dmitri Mikos, bag in hand, emerging from Jeakes House, the bed and breakfast where he had stayed during the festival. The smile on his handsome face was so radiant I thought he must have picked up the habit from Raymond.

"Going back to Athens, Dmitri?"

"Yes, for a week. Then I have bookings in the States. I'll be working with Ilena again in the spring. We do *Traviata* in Nice."

"Yes, I remember. Your career is going well, isn't it?"

"Wonderful! That's all that matters in this life, you know."

I laughed. For so many performers, this was the ultimate creed.

Ten minutes later, I found Raymond Flynt leaving the desk at the Dolphin, where he had settled his bill. We climbed the stairs together and stood on the landing to say goodbye.

White teeth gleaming, he said, "Ilena's packing. It takes her forever."

"Going back to Los Angeles?"

"Yes. We have a flight this afternoon from Heathrow. Not too keen on going there, but what can you do? You and James had a lucky escape."

I nodded. "Will you be glad to be home again?"

"Oh, yes. Time to get back to my practice. I've left it long enough this time."

"How *do* you manage to leave your practice, Raymond?" I had wondered more than once about this but had never had the courage to ask.

"I practice with two other doctors and we arrange the practice so we can fill in for each other. You see, we're not analysts," he concluded, as if that explained everything.

"Not analysts?"

"Right. Those boys are really dinosaurs—you know, the ones who see patients several times a week for years and talk about childhood trauma. Talk therapy is fine for mild neuroses like Ilena's, for instance, but since we've learned about the chemical origins of most so-called mental illnesses, all that talk is baloney for the really serious cases. Now we look for the appropriate medication or other kinds of treatment, and thank God, we're getting results."

I heard the genuine enthusiasm in Raymond's voice, and looking at that beaming smile, I thought I saw what all those wives had been attracted to: there was real warmth in that grin, and for all his idiosyncrasies, when the chips were down, Raymond would be there.

Riccardo's farewell was conducted with typically Italian gusto.

"Jane, my angel! I shall see you again when I am in London!"

"Yes, do, Riccardo. Perhaps you'll see more of your lady from the chorus when you are in England?"

"Ah, alas, it is not likely. Her husband has returned from his business journey abroad. I never wish to come between husband and wife—it is not seemly!"

I wasn't sure it was seemly to make love to the lady when her husband was away, but Riccardo gave me a look of such solemn rectitude that I could only giggle inwardly and praise him for his forbearance.

At Southmere, Bettina worked mechanically at her desk, deep shadows under her eyes. "I must hold up for Simon's sake. He'll need me, Jane."

"Have you seen him this morning?"

"No, but the solicitor recommended by Mr. Kemp talked with me. Simon has decided to plead guilty to the charges and hope for mercy from the court."

"It's his first offense. That may help a bit."

"Yes. At least, Jane, he had nothing to do with Uncle Julian's death. I feel so guilty about this, but the truth is, I was frightened at first that Simon might—well, have done something rash. You see, I knew Uncle Julian had threatened Simon with something, but I had no idea what it was about. I'm glad now that Uncle never knew what it was."

"Bettina, I do hate to ask this, but were Simon and Mick Corcoran involved in the Heathrow bombing?"

"No! It seems to have been another faction of the IRA who were responsible for that, thank heaven. What they have done is bad enough—what with the smuggling and the robbery."

I had wondered if Bettina would at last have felt doubts about Simon, if she might even turn away from a man who could allow himself to be drawn into criminal acts. How could I have doubted? That loyal little heart would never waver, whatever Simon's weaknesses. And one thing was true: in his insubstantial way, Simon truly adored her, and she knew it.

Now she looked at the tray on her desk where I had surreptitiously slipped the third monkey back into its place. "Look, Jane, someone found little Speak No Evil!"

I looked at the three wrinkled faces, dispensing their

ancient Chinese wisdom, and thought that Bettina herself could represent a fourth figure, called "Believe No Evil."

In the end, it was several weeks before the authorities sorted things out and decided how to proceed in the death of Julian Kingsley. The Dan Hawks case, ironically enough, was solved almost at once. The revolver Margot had used to kill Anton had indeed belonged to Simon, as she told Bettina that night. Identified as one of the two handguns taken from Wilkins's shop on the night of the burglary, it provided the proof of Simon's and Mick Corcoran's guilt.

When Dan Hawks was duly released, his mother told James she was sending him to stay with country cousins, away from the bad company he kept in London.

"Fat lot of good that will do," James scoffed. "He'll no doubt corrupt all those innocents in darkest Yorkshire!"

As for the Kingsley murder, the CID officially accepted Anton Szabo as the killer and were able to close the books on that aspect of the crime. There remained the sticky problem of whether or not Margot could be tried as an accessory.

As Detective Chief Inspector Collier told James, "We have her dead to rights on killing Szabo. The evidence on the other charge is much more difficult to prove. The prosecutor for the Crown has decided to take the bird in the hand, so to speak."

I asked James, "Will her barrister plead that she shot Anton in the heat of passion, or whatever they call it?"

"He'll no doubt have a go at it. What else can one say? That ploy often works when a couple are married and the erring spouse is caught in the act, as it were.

Whether it works for a lover who has just murdered one's husband is another matter! I suspect Margot may be in for a long term in prison."

There were some things we would never know. Did Anton really plan to kill me when he lured me to the tower? I thought not. My guess was that when he saw my car, he looked in the theater to see if I had taken shelter there from the storm. Not finding me, he picked up the "Speak No Evil" figure from Bettina's desk, and assuming that I had been sitting in my car and must have seen the two of them emerge from the tower, no doubt kissing passionately again before Margot walked down the hill, decided to give me a warning.

By the same token, was Margot trying to set up James as a suspect in Julian's murder? This seemed more likely. First, there were the requests to see her at her flat in London, allowing the police to believe James tried to make love to her. Then, she knew James was expected to arrive at Southmere that evening, probably assuming it would be considerably after seven o'clock. Of course she couldn't know that he would actually walk up to the tower and find Julian, but the fact that he could have arrived earlier than he claimed would be enough to cast suspicion on him. Even if the evidence wasn't strong enough to convict him, it would draw attention away from the truth.

An amusing grace-note was added to the case by John Kemp, Julian's friend and solicitor. He felt strongly that Julian's money rightfully belonged to Bettina, the niece Julian adored. Kemp pointed out to Margot that if she was tried and convicted of being an accessory to Julian's murder, she would get nothing from the estate. If, however, she turned over a good portion of the money to Bettina, and *if* she was not tried on that charge, she would come out of prison with enough to live in style.

Margot saw the point, and signed over to Bettina the ownership of Southmere as well as many major holdings from the Kingsley millions, thus assuring that the Southmere Festival would be on under Bettina's direction. What effect all this money would have upon Simon when he was finally free was anybody's guess.

"Maybe fatherhood will shape him up," I said to James. For Bettina had learned to her delight that she was pregnant, and Simon had seemed as ecstatic as she at the news.

25

Veeda Riley recovered slowly from her wounds. When I was finally allowed to visit her in the hospital, she told me what had happened the day she was shot.

"When I saw the news on the telly about the bombing at Heathrow, I was terribly afraid Riley was involved, and that he might have drawn my brother into it as well. I didn't know then that Mick and your friend's husband had already been arrested on the smuggling and robbery charges.

"I had known for a long time that Riley was working with a splinter group of the IRA, but I hadn't a shred of proof. That afternoon, he turned up at my flat and asked me to let him stay for a couple of days until the heat was off. There's a false closet with a panel behind it which he had built years ago. He's used it more than once when searches were on.

"He swore he'd had nothing to do with the Heathrow affair, but I didn't believe him. We had a terrible row, and I told him I was really through with the whole mess. I wouldn't protect him—or Mick—any longer, and he stomped out of the flat.

"I was in the bedroom, and I picked up the phone

to ring you. By that time, I was sure those devils had had something to do with Julian's death, and I wanted you to ask your husband's advice about what I might do.

"I should have locked the door after Riley left, but I wasn't thinking straight. Of course, he sneaked back in and heard me on the phone. He thought I was calling the police, and he screamed at me, 'You bitch, you'll never live to tell the coppers anything!' And he shot me."

I said, "I read in the newspapers that your husband was arrested here at the hospital. Is that true?"

"Yes, the bastard. He thought the guard had left his post outside the door, and he came in and tried to strangle me. Actually, the guard was in the corner here in my room behind a screen, and when I screamed, he leaped out and caught Riley in the act.

"He'll be in for a long stretch, thank God. I've decided to sell the shops and go live in the States. I could do with some sunshine. Florida, maybe?"

I smiled, "Why not?"

A week before Christmas, we were packing our suitcases for the flight to Los Angeles, where we would spend the holidays. James had told Andrew on the phone that we were taking him to a gala dinner to celebrate his standing as Sleuth of the Year.

Staring at my half-filled case, I said, "I'm happy for Bettina that she's taking her trouble so well. But I must confess I had rather hoped that if she turned against Simon, Andrew might have queued up for the hand of the fair maiden. He was certainly taken with her."

James laughed. "My dear little matchmaker, has it occurred to you that one day Andrew may find the woman of his dreams without the least help from you?''

The sound of the doorbell deprived me of a just retort.

"There's MacDougal."

James was using MacDougal's services again on a new case, and when the two had finished their conference, I presented the detective with a gaily-wrapped plum pudding as our Christmas offering.

"Thank you very much indeed, Mrs. H."

We chatted for a bit, and when he was about to take his leave, I wondered if we would be favored with a parting squib of Milton. I wasn't disappointed.

James remarked that he was glad Scotland Yard had been called in on the present case.

"Righto." MacDougal stepped toward the door, saying without a quiver, "As we used to say when I was in the force:

> *The CID does all it can*
> *To justify God's ways to man.''*